Fires of Affinity

INTERTWINED SERIES
BOOK TWO

DELIA DUKE

Sign Up

Sign up for the mailing list to be the first to know about new book releases!

WEBSITE
INSTAGRAM
FACEBOOK

Also by the Author

Fate Intertwined – Book One of Intertwined Series

Novella -

A Sultry Betrayal

The heart has its reasons of which reason knows nothing.

– Blaise Pascal

Content Warning

This story contains explicit sexual content, profanity, and topics that may be sensitive to some readers.

Chapter One

The ice hadn't thawed since our fight the night before. Forgiving Nick still felt inconceivable. His unwillingness to admit to his mistakes intensified the divide. Without a word, we dressed in separate rooms within his presidential suite and prepared our belongings. A full continental breakfast of quiches, assorted tarts, scones, eggs, sausages, and bacon in the hotel's dining hall went unnoticed while we lapsed into our own frigid silences, unresolved conflict consuming us. I could hardly focus on anything but the relentless churn of frustration surging through me.

The driver from last night maneuvered through Greater Boston's streets. The tension in the confined space stayed as is. The silence sat thick and heavy as the city, my home for the last four years, blurred past my window. Beside me, Nick stared out, his face impassive, but his hands, clenching and unclenching, betrayed the tension simmering between us. The deafening lull continued through the drive to Hanscom Airfield, a small airstrip I had heard of but never been to until now.

For the next half hour, the hum of the charter plane was my constant companion until we reached our destination: Teterboro, New Jersey.

Nick and I didn't so much as glance at each other. He glued himself to his laptop while I skimmed through Branson Capital's brochure—a publicly traded company with a global presence—managing portfolios, developing real estate, running hospitality ventures, and supporting charitable initiatives. The list seemed endless.

When we reached outside the Branson Capital's private hangar, a heavy-bearded pilot approached us. He shook Nick's hand and then mine, an unusually soft hand for a large and muscular man. His build was that of a seasoned football linebacker. If not for his white suit with the Branson logo sewn onto his lapel, I wouldn't have thought of him as a pilot at all. Yes, I paid attention to every detail, desperate to keep my mind occupied.

Nick and the captain walked with me over the wide-open and deserted airstrip. Their discussion about aeronautical technicalities and wind speed filled the silence, while I continued to nurse my bruised heart.

We approached a navy-blue helicopter. The propeller blades created their own wind, and the roar sent a rumbling sensation through my chest. I reminded myself it had nothing to do with the man beside me.

The pilot waved us over to get on. Nick held the door for me and extended his hand. I took it without thinking, but my body reacted differently. Electricity coursed through my veins, waking my desires instantly.

He waited a second too long before letting go of my hand and then he joined me inside the helicopter. After putting on his own noise-canceling headphones, Nick helped me with mine. The warmth and familiarity of his touch started to melt my heart. It took everything inside me not to lean into his hand and give in.

"*You good*?" Nick's voice filtered through my headphones.

His question was directed towards the setting of my headphones. *No, I am not,* I thought, but I nodded and slumped back into my seat. Exasperated, my left hand dropped to the space between us.

"*All set, Miss McAlister?*" I heard the pilot's voice through the headphones. He must've thought it was an everyday occurrence for me to hop into a helicopter and fly from one city to another. Reality was far from that.

"*Ready for takeoff,*" the pilot announced.

"Where is this thing going to land?" I asked, barely able to hide the tension I felt from Nick's little finger being on mine. I deliberately didn't withdraw my hand to prove he had no effect on me.

I burned for him.

The pilot said a string of sentences. I only understood "*Branson Capital.*" Honestly, it didn't matter, I could even go to hell with this man. Nick, the man of my dreams, who all my desires centered on, yet somehow remained the bane of my life.

Our ride was uneventful, mostly because I forced myself not to forget last night. In less than ten minutes, we were circling over Branson Capital's headquarters in downtown Manhattan. Mesmerized by the uninterrupted clear blue skies above us and the concrete jungle below, New York City welcomed me once again. The thrill and excitement of coming back home buzzing inside me. As soon as we landed and it was safe to get out, I planted my feet on solid ground and started walking toward the shiny aluminum door and into Nick's powerhouse from where he ruled the world.

Nick was quick. His lithe body, clad in a black suit, moved in front of me, all hard muscle blocking my way, making me stop, and then he tried to peck my lips. At over six feet, he literally had to bend down to level with me, standing at his shoulder height in flat shoes.

I turned away. The kiss landed on my cheek. Our battle of wills continued.

He took my hand as we moved forward. "How long are you planning to fight over ridiculous things?"

"As long as it takes for you to accept your mistake." I turned to him, holding his gaze and ignoring the trepidation in my heart.

"I'll not apologize, Ivy, if that's what you're hoping for."

"It's too late for apologies, don't you think?" I retorted. If he thought I would cower and take his bullshit, he had another thing coming.

Our staring contest continued until the chopper flew away. Going all alpha-male on me and treating me like a possession in front of my ex-boyfriend—with whom I had broken up exactly twenty-four hours previously—was not acceptable.

Letting go of my hand, Nick opened the heavy metal door. Once I was inside and he was no longer quite so near, I breathed again. He always had that effect on me—an irresistible pull, irrespective of our circumstance.

Inside the welcoming silence of the concrete walls, I took the stairs without waiting for him. Another door opened a level below us, and I saw the man who had removed my bag from the helicopter go inside. I wasn't sure where he was going. I wasn't used to people doing things for me. It was as if I had stepped out of my Boston apartment last night and into someone else's world.

"Were you always feisty, or is that something new you picked up at Harvard?" Nick asked, catching up to me.

"You have no idea what you got yourself into," I responded to his absurdity.

He ignored it, of course. "Let's go to my office. My meeting doesn't start for another thirty minutes."

"Find someone else to fill those thirty minutes. I'm going home." Before I rounded the corner to take the next flight of stairs, Nick caught my elbow and wrapped me up in his arms. I didn't move, denying him the satisfaction of my reaction. Every bone in my body was screaming his name, forcing me to give in and end the madness right now.

He broke the silence. "Stop fighting. Mike is old news. It's not like you're ever going to see him again."

"That's not the point, Nick. What happened last night was wrong."

"What's happening between us is wrong." His gaze bore down on my eyes, challenging me to say otherwise.

I looked sideways. Being in his presence turned me into putty, but I wasn't ready to give in. I didn't want him to interfere in my personal life. Period.

Nick didn't understand me, and it was freaking frustrating, but I also didn't want to start our first day back in New York with the same fight. It was bad enough we'd argued in the first place, and I slept in the guest bedroom of his suite.

Our relationship was brand new. There was a lot we still didn't know about each other. And who was I kidding? I wanted *us* to work. Nick was the only one I'd ever wanted, more than anything or anyone else in the world.

"Let's meet in the evening," I capitulated, my voice softer now.

"Six, at my place?"

"That works."

Annoyed by my resistance, he closed the distance and kissed my cheek. This time, I let him. He didn't move back, asserting what this attraction meant to both of us. Honestly, it was impossible to ignore the chemistry between us when we were sticking together like magnets. I didn't retract until he released me, reluctantly.

Fingers entwined, we resumed our walk together. "John will take you home. I'll see you off," he said, with a hint of disappointment.

"No to both. I'll take the subway home." John? Another driver, perhaps. I only knew Tom well enough since he had been with Nick as long as I could remember. His personal chauffeur and bodyguard, combined into one.

Nick halted. Since we were holding hands, I did too. "Ivy, you can't say no to everything."

"Is that so?" I countered, but couldn't argue. We were here to give this relationship a chance. Even though I wanted my independence, I wanted him equally if not more. I could continue our fight or move forward, and I chose the latter. "All right. John can take me home. See you in the evening."

———

THE CITY HADN'T CHANGED IN THE LAST THREE DAYS, but my emotional state sure had. I left heartbroken on a Saturday night and returned ambivalent on a Wednesday morning. To say the least, my life had been an emotional rollercoaster ever since I'd reconnected with Nick.

Today, just like me, Manhattan was alive, vibrant, and pulsating with energy. I wanted to be part of the bustling crowds again, to feel the vigor and zest this city offered. Instead, I was in the backseat of Nick's Lincoln Navigator.

After dropping me off at the McAlister building on the Upper West Side, Nick's driver, Mr. Serious John—a nickname I'd given him because he never cracked a smile—waited until I had safely walked inside.

Doug, the building manager, greeted me with a warm smile

as soon as I entered. He had known me since birth and had been there for me after the death of my parents. He had walked the cops to our door when they'd come to tell us about the accident, and he was the only one who understood my untamed anger that had followed.

Life had toughened me up since then. I didn't get as angry anymore. Neither did I get sad. I learned that life went on no matter what. Now I channeled all the negative energy into something healthy.

I ran. Who needs a gym when you can use the entire city as your personal running track?

"Miss McAlister. It's always a pleasure to see you."

"One of these days, I'll get you to stop calling me that." I smiled and gave Doug a warm hug. "How are you?"

"Never better!"

He helped me hoist my bag up the two steps and then rolled it over to the elevator. My late father had bought this posh Renaissance building before I was born, and since then it had been the residence of the McAlister family. We had made a home here, a happy one, until our parents' demise. For the last few years, only Ryan had been living in the penthouse. Now that he was engaged, his fiancée, Risha, lived here, too.

"I've some packages for Mr. Ryan. Would you like me to send them up to the penthouse?" Doug asked, reminding me of a day-old message from my brother.

"That would be great. Thanks, Doug," I told him, smiling back.

———

By the time I reached the highest floor of the building, a porter, not much older than me, was already at the door with a bell cart full of parcels. I quickly removed my phone from the back pocket of my jeans and texted Ryan as I rolled my bag from the elevator.

Hi Big Brother! Do you have an online shopping addiction I don't know about? I get to your house and there are like thirty packages here.

I exaggerated, of course, and let the man in as my phone chimed.

Welcome back!!! No to the shopping addiction. Most are engagement presents sent to our home. And stop with that "your house" nonsense. It's as much yours as it is mine. It was followed by a couple of angry devil emojis.

I texted back, **Fine. I relinquish my share. Think of it as a gift to my favorite couple.** Now that I had moved back to Manhattan, I needed a place of my own. It was the very first item added to my to-do list.

You know what would be a perfect gift? You joining McAlister Group.

Not again, Ryan.

I ignored him long enough for him to send me a follow-up text. ***Our discussion is still pending. Let's talk when I return.***

I should've bitten the bullet, called him, and said what I had to say in that very moment. **Looking forward to it. Say hi to Risha.**

I couldn't. I knew I would never join him. Delivering that message was a different story altogether.

His message popped up again, **Will do! Enjoy home.**

Once all the packages were inside, I locked the front door and headed straight to my teenage bedroom, frozen in time from eight years ago—all soft purple walls and white furniture from my mother's favorite furniture store. My taste had changed a lot over the years, but the pieces still held memories of my parents. It was sweet of Ryan to leave my room as is during the big renovation and allow me to hold on to the pieces of their memories for just a bit longer.

With nothing else to do for the rest of the day, I found the business card Professor Sinclair had handed me at MoxTo's opening last Friday. I called her and she picked up on the third ring. I introduced myself, half-expecting her to not have a clue who I was, but she recognized me right away.

"I just sent you my address. Come see me!" she said, right as my phone chimed.

The Dr. Gwen Sinclair was giving me her precious time? "I'm on my way," I responded, talking fast before she changed her mind.

Chapter Two

I entered Columbia University through the main wrought-iron gates, trying to get a feel for the campus. The pylons, the architecture, and the lawns where I could see myself studying for hours. In a way, the place reminded me of Harvard.

And a pang of guilt hit me right in the chest. This was never part of my plan. My dream was to continue my study at Harvard.

Other than Harvard and Nick, you had no dreams. Unfortunately, they don't fit into the same picture, so you adjusted the frame. Now, try to be happy with your decision and hope that Columbia takes you in.

Disheartened and still not over last night's argument with Nick, I pulled my phone out of my oversized jute tote. A text message was waiting for me from "Love."

How is your day going so far? Miss me at all?

I checked the previous messages from the same number and concluded that "Love" was Nick. On our date yesterday, he had saved his numbers on my phone and apparently this was the best name he could come up with.

But I was still fighting with him. I typed and deleted five times before I sent **Nick, right?** I wasn't ready to let things go yet.

His response came almost immediately. ***How many people send you messages that you never recognize me? It is Nick. The one and only.***

I was already on the second floor and right in front of Professor Sinclair's office when I finished typing my response. **Next time, save your name to avoid such confusion. Gotta go.** I knew the message would give him food for thought, given what name he'd saved his number under. Satisfaction went through me.

I dropped my phone into the tote. My full attention shifted to the person I could see through the gap in the door.

Professor Sinclair sat behind her desk, eyes on her screen. With her inky black hair and light brown eyes, she possessed a mature beauty. I would be lucky to look half as beautiful as her when I was her age. She was twice-divorced because her work always came first—that was public knowledge among the students. Her younger daughter was around my age, but she wasn't at Harvard. Both of her kids had chosen universities in England to be closer to their father and to Gwen's first ex-husband.

Growing up, most girls admired celebrities or athletes and aspired to be like them one day. Professor Gwen Sinclair was that role model for me. One of the most renowned professors in the country, she was all about empowering women in the business world. Over the last few years, I had attended almost all her seminars. Her confidence, self-assurance, and powerful speeches about paving your own way in life... it was electric.

I was over the moon when I'd been given a spot in her class

at the Harvard Business School, only to find out last week that she had moved to Columbia.

I knocked lightly on the door. "Good morning, Professor Sinclair."

She looked up from her laptop, eyes glimmering behind her white, square-rimmed glasses. "Ivy! Come on in. And please, call me Gwen. No need to be so formal."

Was I on a first-name basis with *the* Gwen Sinclair? I didn't understand what I had done to deserve this honor, but I embraced it. "Gwen. Hi." I stepped inside the room and walked the last five steps to her desk.

She nodded, extending a warm smile. "Much better! Please, sit. How does it feel being in New York?"

"I love the energy." I got comfortable in one of the two padded leather chairs. Her desk was sleek, minimalist, and L-shaped with drawers. "Very different from Boston, though."

"Isn't it? You're young and bright, I'm sure it won't take long for you to adjust."

"You're probably right. I'm sorry for not calling you earlier in the week. Time sort of got away from me." With everything going on in my personal life, calling her on Monday completely slipped my mind.

"Don't sweat it. Just tell me this: Did you decide about Columbia?"

Her question caught me off guard. I sat up straight, rewinding and repeating her question in my head again. The decision wasn't exactly mine. Columbia University had to accept me. That meant I had to apply first. "Honestly, I'm hoping to see if I could transfer, but I'm pretty sure I missed the MBA application deadline."

"I'm glad you're considering it. I've already spoken to Rob and he has only good things to say about you. I don't see any reason why we couldn't make an exception for an exceptional student."

"You spoke with Professor Robert Baldacci about me?" My eyeballs popped in disbelief. Literally. My undergrad professor at Harvard, Robert Baldacci, was also my mentor and the one who suggested I should try to get into Gwen's class.

"I sure did. If you want the spot at Columbia, it's yours."

My heart raced, but not out of panic. It was another level of excitement. "I don't know what to say…"

"Say *yes*." She smiled to compensate for my disbelieving to bewildered expression. "I know I'm going too fast, but how do you feel about assisting me on a couple of projects I'm consulting on? It'll be a great learning experience for you, and I could definitely use an extra set of eyes and hands."

I was nothing short of shell-shocked. "Are–are you asking me to be your assistant?"

"Yes, Ivy. That's exactly what I'm asking you."

Was this my lucky day or what?

My brain was still processing our conversation, but she kept going. "The fall semester is right around the corner. I need time to concentrate on class prep. I also do consultations for corporations and all of them require a lot of my time and attention," she explained. "You come highly recommended, so I thought I could use your skills. Shadow me. Assist me. Then, in a few months, when you're ready, you can take the lead on a project of your choice. How does that sound?"

"I would love that very much!" I could no longer conceal my joy. Smile oozed out of every pore of my face.

"Great. Just so you know, the pay won't be what you would earn at a corporate level. But I can involve you in as many projects as you'd like."

"I'll take it, Gwen. Pay is not an issue."

With the McAlister fortune backing me, I never had to

work for money. Ryan had always made sure my bank account had more than I could ever spend. There was also a large trust fund my parents had set aside for me on the day I was born. So far, I hadn't used a single dollar out of it and it had multiplied exponentially by now. Ryan thought the trust fund was peanuts compared to the McAlister Group's current market value and he might be right, but I also knew my next two generations could live off of that trust fund if they had to.

Boston had changed my lifestyle. I didn't splurge often, and when I did, it was only on clothes and accessories. Thanks to the influence of my late mother, Sarah McAlister, I took my appearance seriously.

Gwen smiled again, showing off her beautiful laugh lines. "That's what I thought. Now tell me: How soon can you start? I needed somebody yesterday."

"Today, tomorrow... I'm yours whenever you need me." The opportunity of my life and it had literally just fallen in my lap. I knew professors invited students to shadow them, but they only chose the cream of the crop. I never considered myself to be part of that pool, though Professor Baldacci would beg to differ. I also knew I was still green with not enough experience under my belt. I had a long road ahead of me.

Assisting Dr. Gwen Sinclair and getting to pick her brain was more than I had asked for or dreamed of, and it was actually happening! In real life!

"You probably want to have some fun before school starts again in the fall. I would hate myself if I interrupted any of your summer plans. Take as much time off as you need and keep me posted on when you can start."

"I don't have any plans as of now, but that works."

"Good." Gwen got up from her chair. "In that case, the only thing left is to get you enrolled."

I was downright giddy as I followed her to the other side of the campus, where she introduced me to a few people at the registrar's office. They helped me fill out a bunch of forms; took the documents that I had, by chance, decided to bring with me; and promised to expedite the transfer process. Unlike Harvard, the staff members at Columbia were eager to help. I couldn't help but notice their less uptight and more friendly behavior. After everything was done, all I had to do was call Harvard and have the university transfer my credits.

Two and a half hours later, exhausted yet elated, I went back to Gwen's office to tell her I was all set. We agreed to meet tomorrow morning and said our goodbyes.

———

By the time I reached the subway station, the place was swarming with people everywhere. Overcrowded platforms made it impossible to cut to the front without pushing through a sea of bodies. I stood a respectful distance away from the edge of the platform—so I wouldn't get pushed or accidentally fall onto the tracks—and realized that I was once again becoming a true New Yorker. When the train pulled into the station, I leapt inside before the doors closed on me, and then stood in a corner because empty seats were impossible to find.

Boston offered me a calmer lifestyle that I loved, but the palpable energy of Manhattan was exhilarating. I felt alive after so many years of simply existing instead of living.

Once I got off at my station, I rummaged through my tote and pulled out my phone. I was bursting with excitement and needed to share the good news with someone before I exploded.

I sent the first text to Abby, my best friend and closest confidante. **Guess what? Not only did I officially transfer** to Columbia, but Professor Sinclair hired me as her assistant. I'm starting tomorrow!

Her response came immediately. *OMG! Are you serious??? Didn't I tell you risks comes with rewards.*

I smiled so much that people around me probably thought I was high on something. And I was. Happiness.

I'm falling back in love with this city, that's for sure. This is my dream come true. Yesterday was a disaster though. I can't get over it. Was Mike okay after we left?

He'll be fine. Don't blame yourself for what happened.

Abby's response didn't make me feel any better. Nick's domineering, controlling nature had no bounds. Sometimes he truly had no regard for other people's feelings.

I can never forgive myself for what happened. Mike didn't deserve that.

Talk to Nick when things cool down. Explain yourself without getting upset. That's the only way to get your point across.

She spoke my mind because being upset wasn't getting us anywhere. And getting upset was my biggest weakness. Or, at least it used to be before I moved to Boston. Unfortunately, as soon as I returned, so did my old habits. Wanting to change the subject, I texted back.

How are things on your end?

Great! Update: I put up ads for the furniture and my phone is already blowing up.

My sudden decision to move to Manhattan had left Abby responsible for selling all the furniture at our Boston apartment. Guilty for dumping all the work on her, I replied.

You're the best. I owe you big time.

Bring your ass back before I leave. That's all you owe me.

She was crazy if she thought I wouldn't be there to see her off. Best friends and roommates since our freshmen year, we were friends for life. I was glad I'd had the time to pack some of our boxes yesterday while my brain and heart tussled between the comfort of contentment or the chaos of love, known and safe or a pull that never left my heart.

My mind gave in to my heart's demand.

On my walk back to the apartment, I took Abby's advice. Putting a pause on yesterday's disagreement, I texted Nick.

How's your day going? I can't wait to share some news. Btw, where do you live?

Dots immediately popped up on my phone screen. ***Looking forward to hearing all about it. Day has been crazy. Heading into a meeting now, will call you after.***

The man had literally missed two days of work because of me. Pretty sure he was still catching up.

After spending a day around Nick, which led to the most mind-blowing sex of my life, I had thought he was done with me. Heartbroken, I left the city with no way for him to get in touch with me. When he found me forty-eight hours later, we both confessed our feelings to each other. And now here I was, ready to give our relationship a chance and find out where this feeling would lead us.

My dreams were quickly transforming into reality. Moving back truly was the best decision I had ever made.

Chapter Three

After getting out of the shower, I put on a soft-pink chiffon dress, paired it with gold hoop earrings, and let my hair hang down my back. The color was my own natural brown, and it gleamed after I blow-dried it, styled it prettily. My nude-colored wedges gave me the sensation of walking in the clouds. I also needed that extra height if I wanted to stand beside Nick.

On my way out, I opened Nick's text message and found his address—which ended with a red heart. Smiling profusely and rubbing my thumb over the silly red emoji, I got inside the elevator ready to meet my *Love*.

In the lobby downstairs, I waved to Doug, who was busy talking to a resident of this building carrying a poodle in her arms. I crossed the marble floor and opened the glass door. The moment I stepped out of my building, Nick's arms wrapped around me. One arm around my shoulders, and the other slung around my waist, I felt wanted. My body was electrified, and my skin throbbed from his heat.

Electricity crackled between us and ignited a fire within my heart. His eyes warmed with a mixture of wanting and ache, gaze explained unspoken words, reflecting something that ran deeper than our physical attraction.

Without waiting for my permission, Nick's lips claimed mine. Tongue sliding against my own, he explored my mouth as if we hadn't met in years. I surrendered to this relentless torture. Pleasurable. Gratifying. *I belong here.*

His other hand held me firmly close to him. I wrapped my arms around his neck, enjoying the moment. And enjoying Nick. The distance between us was hurting me now. I needed this. I had needed him my whole life.

My fingers threaded through his silky brown hair. Lifting up onto my tiptoes, my tongue slid deeper into his mouth, satisfying my own need. Our tongues rolled in unison as they danced the tango. My racing heartbeat reverberated in my ear, drawing out the rest of the world and recalling the intensity of our passion.

The minutes went by, fighting for dominance of our kiss. Then the catcalling started.

"Get a room!" a passerby yelled, reminding us we were right there, on the street. My eyes caught a few pedestrians giving us appreciative looks before two grumpy grinches passed by. Public display of affection wasn't my thing until this moment.

Nick pulled away. I took the opportunity to admire his beautiful face—the angular, artfully sculpted lips were half open in a smile, sharp jawline, and eyes filled with exuberance. His mused hair was my doing, though. "Were we supposed to meet here?" I asked to break the spell.

"I couldn't wait." He took my hand, and we started walking shoulder to shoulder.

The city bustled around us, the chatter of people filling up the street. We walked to the end of the block and stopped in front of a tall, white-stoned building with double glass doors.

"We're practically neighbors," I giggled. "Have you always lived here?" I couldn't believe the proximity of our places.

"Ever since I fell for you."

"Seriously? You moved here five days ago?" Because that was exactly when I shattered my resolve and returned to Manhattan. Meeting Nick was equal part chance and destiny.

"Smartass. That should be your middle name."

The doorman opened the door and stepped aside for us to go through. Paying no attention to him, Nick turned to me and continued. "I told you, Ivy. My feelings didn't appear overnight. I've wanted you forever."

"You've been pining after me since I was born, then?" I asked, feigning seriousness.

He rolled his eyes so high I feared it would get stuck behind his head. "Like I said, you're a real smartass."

I laughed. I had missed him. All these years of waiting and wanting and hoping that the feelings were mutual were finally paying off.

Nick touched the corner of my lips like he wanted a piece of my smile. Putting one hand behind his head, I pulled his face closer and gave him a slow, deep kiss, seductive in its languidness. After I got my fill, Nick soon took the lead. His tongue sank deeper, giving in to all the restraint he had showed since last night. When we released each other, we were both blushing. Nick's dimple prominent as he smiled. My own face flushed with warmth. "Seriously, I didn't know you lived so close," I told him.

"Now we have all the time in the world to get to know each other." Nick took my hand before we stepped forward. The doorman again opened the door for us and this time, we didn't make him wait but started walking straight into the high rise. "You've no idea how happy your decision has made me."

"Me too." My cheeks burned. "I wanted this more than I was ready to admit."

"That's what I wanted to hear."

"I'm assuming you own this building?" I asked. The brochure on Brandon Capital mentioned a substantial part of Manhattan's real estate was owned by them without going into the specifics.

"For almost a decade now. This was one of my personal purchases," he explained. "Though the credit goes to Ryan. His business acumen on real estate and hospitality was mind boggling. I was learning from him."

"And then you beat him..." in terms of valuation. Nick knew exactly what I was saying because he chuckled as we walked past the glass door.

"Only because I have more cash to spend. He is still smarter than me," Nick said modestly.

I crossed the threshold and walked into the lobby of his building. The world around me changed. Furniture, fixtures, and even the security desk had a more modern touch to them compared to the gilded décor in the McAlister building where Ryan and I reside. Nick inserted a keycard once we got into the rightmost elevator and we started ascending.

He didn't stop looking at me. I couldn't stop blushing. Happiness radiated from every pore of my skin.

"What's going on?" Nick placed a stray strand of hair behind my ear and snaked his arms around my waist. My improved mood was reflected in his.

"I've never been to your place before." I was excited to see where he lived, how he lived. So little did I know about this man, and I left my entire life behind to be with him. Five days was all it took to change the whole trajectory of my life and leave Boston, Harvard, and Mike to be with the man of my dreams.

The elevator stopped on the top floor. "Let's check it out, then."

With our fingers entwined, we stepped into a large foyer that was also the entrance to his penthouse suite. Contemporary to the core, this place was nothing short of modern art. A gigantic vase with dried black and white flowers dominated the foyer. Pristine marble floors, white walls with uneven paintings, and strategically placed lights to keep the focus on the walls screamed luxury.

Through the archway of the foyer, we entered an enormous open living space with a glass floor-to-ceiling wall in front of us. Beyond the glass was a sizable terrace decorated with oversized furniture. The wide, picturesque New York landscape splayed out like a photograph.

I walked further in. A formal dining room was on my left and next to it was a very modern open kitchen with every cooking gadget one could imagine. The apartment oozed opulence, but it bore no resemblance to his parents' house that was more like a home to me. Standing there, it was like I had stepped into a museum.

I turned to him. "Is this house decorated to your taste?"

"You don't like it?"

"It's different. Nothing like your parents' house. Somehow, I never imagined you in something like this." I waved my hand, once again taking in the place's vibe. The abstract art pieces were enticing, with colors seamlessly flowing into one another. The house cried out for attention, for every piece had been chosen to fit the theme of dominance and sophistication. But it lacked the warmth and familiarity of a home.

"And yet you think you don't know me," Nick teased.

Our eyes met. I must've started blushing because my cheeks burned. I looked away.

His kitchen had a big skylight overhead, providing a decent amount of light, even in the evening. "Your kitchen, though… someone might mistake you for a chef."

"Looks can be deceiving," Nick chuckled.

Honestly, expecting him to make a cup of coffee would be an overstretch. He must've had people doing all the work for him.

Hallways on both sides led to other rooms, I assumed, but it was the terrace that was calling my name. Seamless sliding doors automatically opened when I was a few feet away.

Skirting around the furniture, I made my way to the glass parapet with steel dividers and soaked in the city's beauty—captivating, mesmerizing, a world within itself. Undoubtedly, this was one of the tallest buildings on the Upper West Side. Below us, the lush and beautiful Central Park mapped out, vast and beautiful. From my vantage point, I could see people taking pictures on Bow Bridge. They looked like tiny ants from here.

His penthouse covered the entire top floor of the building, giving a complete sense of privacy. Unless someone was flying in a chopper, it was impossible to see onto the terrace. Nick must've felt safe here, and so should I.

He walked up to me and handed me a martini glass. It held a cosmo—my new guilty pleasure.

As new as my romance with my teenage crush.

I took the first sip of cold alcohol and swirled it around in my mouth before my eyes returned to the breathtaking scenery below me. "It's beautiful here. I love your terrace."

"Glad you approve of something," he said teasingly, and we clinked our glasses together. "To new beginnings."

"To new beginnings," I echoed, my mind going back to our unresolved argument.

He seemed excited to be here with me, but I couldn't fully immerse myself into this moment until we confronted some mistakes. I got up on my toes and gave him a soft kiss on the cheek. Nick turned his back on the city, giving me his undivided attention. His smile broadened, a beautiful dimple forming on his right cheek.

I took his drink from him and set our glasses down on the nearby table. His expression shifted, understanding exactly where I was going.

"Can we please talk about yesterday?"

"You won't let it go, will you?" His lips pursed into a thin line.

"Unfortunately, I can't. How can we have a new beginning until we sort out our past?" Nick stayed quiet, which gave me a chance to speak my mind. "It was completely wrong of you to treat Mike that way."

"Ivy, when it comes to you, I'm a very possessive man. Knowing you spent an entire evening with another man, kissing him, my blood still boils when I think about it."

His jaws clenched, but he forced himself to control the rage that the memory incited. I knew that feeling all too well; I had gone through similar ones myself. The only difference was that I had run away even though what he had done was nothing compared to how I had spent the evening with Mike.

"There was no way I wouldn't let him know you're mine," Nick said.

"I was his girlfriend then."

"I can't stand you being someone else's girlfriend when you belong to me."

"You know how badly I react when you are with someone

else, too, but I won't hurt anyone because of how I feel. All that has changed now. We're together, and I'm all yours."

He pressed his back to the metal and glass, his gaze fixed on me. He kept his hands shoved into his pockets, restraining himself from touching me. "I like to have control, Ivy, and around you I... I feel like I've lost control."

As the depth of his words sank in, I smiled, taking in his admission. "Believe me, the feeling is mutual. Your presence consumes me, my desires run wild. But I also have a life that doesn't revolve around you, and it shouldn't. Otherwise, I'll lose my identity. Promise me you will let me handle things on my own, with no interference."

In one quick motion, his hands were on my elbow and he was pulling me into his chest. His tongue claimed my mouth, the same powerful force which left me breathless every time. Today, it rose inside me with a kind of madness.

"I'm wrapped around your little finger," he told me, lips moving against mine. "You pull the strings, and I dance. Only you have the power to make me a better man, sweetheart. Or to destroy me."

"And you know how to tug at my heartstrings, say the words I always wanted to hear."

"These are not just words, Ivy. You own me; it's only fair I own a small part of you."

He gave me a heart-melting smile. I moved my lips over the dimple in his cheek, kissing it slowly, roaming further above, and then nipped the tip of his sharp nose.

"Ouch! What was that for?"

"Just because," I said playfully.

"Hmm, is that so?" His smile broadened, mirroring my excitement. "Looks like someone is finally happy."

"You make me happy. And there is one more thing that's making me very happy right now."

"I can't wait to hear what I am competing with." He handed back my glass before picking up his own and waited for what I had to say.

"I met Professor Sinclair today."

He paused for a moment, staring in shock. "I thought you were leaving it to me."

Was my imagination playing tricks, or did he sound displeased? I had always relied on my own hard work to get something. The idea of Nick getting me into Columbia didn't feel right.

"I was going to leave it to you," I continued, "but then I remembered I was supposed to call her earlier this week. When we spoke in the morning, she asked me to come over. One thing led to another." I gave him a quick rundown of what we talked about, and how I had already submitted the paperwork for the transfer, and the assistant job I landed with her.

Nick relaxed noticeably and kissed the crown of my head. Whatever irritation he had was converted into joy.

"This is great, sweetheart. Congratulations! You're one of the smartest women I know. Gwen was wise to pluck you up as soon as you moved here."

"And you know that because Gwen hired me, or because I'm transferring from Harvard?" I laughed at his premature assumptions.

"Sweetheart, I haven't met many women who can hold an intelligent conversation, let alone get into Harvard or Columbia. You have beauty and a brain. And I'm lucky that out of all the men, you chose me."

Sweetheart. I loved the way the word rolled out of his mouth. Endearment and love. Care and adoration. Affection. My entire world was encapsulated into that one word: *sweetheart.*

"You've always been my first choice, Nick. All you had to do was ask." I winked and his smile broadened.

Surreal was not even close to how I felt. Standing there, with the man of my dreams, starting a new job with the person I admired all these years, moving back to the city I left so many years ago... everything was happening too fast, too soon. Life was too perfect.

It can all fall apart at any moment.

Ugh, don't ruin the moment. Bad things don't happen to good people. My parents' sudden death was an anomaly.

"When do you start?" He came closer, taking another sip from his crystal glass and pulling me out of my skepticism.

"Tomorrow morning at eight," I said, grinning like an idiot.

"What?" He flinched. "I thought you would have time until your school began."

"And what do you think we're doing right now?" I cocked my head mischievously.

A hint of irritation returned to his forefront before he covered it swiftly and whisked me in his arms, claiming my mouth again. Whisky mixed with the scent of Nick filled me to the brim. Was he still trying to forget my kiss with Mike, or was he making up for lost time? I couldn't tell, but I loved the wild rush.

"You are mine." His voice was soft, careful.

My heart rate spiked.

His lips trailed down my neck, leaving soft kisses in their wake. The air around us thickened. A burst of wildfire enveloped me, reminding me how reality felt around Nick.

"I missed you all day," he murmured into my ear, before his tongue rolled over my earlobe. "Did you miss me at all?"

"Y... yes." The word emerged in a ragged whisper. The

unrelenting torture of his soft mouth stirred up a throbbing pain down in my belly.

He kissed my chest, my throat, my chin, until our mouths met again. His hand caressed my breast, one at a time, his fingers gently teasing my nipples through my dress. My senses heightened. Each stroke was electrifying, pushing and pulling the air between us and leaving it pulsating. It made me acutely aware that I was exactly where I wanted to be. In his house, in his arms, in Manhattan. Living mt dream.

He withdrew himself abruptly, causing me to recoil. I was deprived of his touch, the only thing I desired. He sat on the circular daybed before me.

"Then prove it," he challenged.

Confusion filled me as I walked over to him. I raised his chin with my finger until our eyes locked again. His dark gaze seared into me, searching for answers.

"I need to know you want me as much as I want you," he said.

Seriously? How could he question my feelings when I had taken this huge leap of faith? Leaving behind my whole world, I had willingly uprooted myself to be with him. I had left behind the comfort of my home, the security of my routine, and the people who had known me for years, all for the chance to be with him. What further proof could he possibly need?

Weren't my actions enough to convince him of the depth of my feelings? Doubt lingered in his eyes. I yearned to erase it, to show him he was the sole occupant of my heart.

"I've been running after you since we met," he reminded me, halting my thoughts.

"And I left everything I know to be with you."

"You think you're the only one who has a lot to lose? I've a lot at stake, as well."

"Oh, yeah? Like what?" I challenged him.

All the doubt left his face, but the smile never returned. "It doesn't matter. I would risk everything just to be with you."

I was taken aback by his claim... his half-baked, half-cryptic admission. It was my turn, but I didn't know how I could possibly prove that my feelings for him spanned a lifetime. Every breath I took, every beat of my heart, whispered his name. He was ingrained in every fiber of my being. I had dreamed of him ever since my hormones ran wild, and my desires had only grown stronger with time. But words seemed insufficient to convey the intensity of these feelings, as if they were too fleeting, too transient.

I took off my dress and tossed it aside before sinking to my knees on the marble floor. My fingers hovered over his thighs. I wanted to prove my feelings for him.

"That's not what I meant," he said.

"What proof are you looking for, Nick? I am starting over my life to be with you." I ran my hand over his growing bulge before I unzipped his jeans.

His eyes, like a pair of deep emerald pools, simmered with an intense thirst. The air crackled with anticipation, as if electricity permeated the atmosphere. A magnetic force had taken hold, drawing us closer and igniting a fire within.

"You're mine too," I uttered. "As much as I'm yours."

I bent down and licked the length of his throbbing shaft before I grazed him with my teeth and lips. Greedy with lust, I tried to get his jeans out of the way. He scooted up to help me, his eyes filled with need. Bending over him, I took him into my mouth and went up and down his erection. The warmth of his thick veins throbbed beneath the cool touch of my tongue, the lingering sensation of the ice from the drink adding a tantalizing contradiction.

When I drew back, his head glistened with pre-cum and my saliva, turning me on. I shivered, wanting more. Wanting it all.

A loud growl escaped his mouth, and I was desperate to please him.

"This would be a good time to stop, so we could talk," I heard him say between his irregular breath, but I ignored him.

His velvety head rolled into my mouth. I sucked him, stroking what I couldn't fit with my fist. Ragged sounds tore through his throat, making me bolder with every passing minute. His sounds were my cues, telling me what to do.

I was on a new adventure.

Nick didn't touch me or force me. He let me take the lead. I placed one hand on his thigh, first moving it sensually and then pressing it hard to cope with my own bubbling desires. I craved him, but I wanted him to understand what he meant to me. I showed him in the only way possible, taking him deeper inside. My mouth glided up and down, repeating the motion until he grunted with pleasure.

A primal growl escaped him before the first burst of thick cum hit the back of my throat. It continued, one release after another, until he had nothing more to give. I took it all because he belonged to me, now and forever.

His head fell back, his breathing heavy and labored. He called out my name in a ragged breath. I licked the remnants of his drops from my lips before rising to my feet. His eyes turned dark, in the deepest shade of grass on a warm summer afternoon, filled with lust and hunger.

"My first," I told him and walked away.

I had only crossed half the terrace when Nick came up from behind, picked me up, and set me down on the lounge chair closest to us. "You didn't have to do that."

"You didn't like it?" Doubt started creeping in. Now that I thought about it, I wasn't sure why I had done that. He would have had so many women before me and they all must've been better.

"Stop second-guessing yourself, Ivy. I want you. I won't forget my first, with you." Nick sat on the floor by my feet. "Do you even know how long I've wanted you?"

"How long?" My heart started drumming in my ears. I wanted to know how long, because I had waited forever to be with Nick.

Rather than responding, his scorching gaze roamed over me. A moan slipped past my lips when his fingers touched the lacy edge of my panties. Pushing his thumb under, Nick dragged them down. He touched the scar on my ankle for a second too long. Kissing my feet and making his way up my calves, my knees, my thighs, his mouth finally pushed between my legs that fell open shamelessly.

"You don't have to reciprocate," I whispered.

His hands went under my ass, pulling me closer to his mouth. "You think I feel any differently about you? I want you, Ivy. Not a part of you, but all of you."

Nick's head went down and he started pleasuring me with his tongue and his mouth. Sucking me, kissing me, taking me to new heights. His expert thumb started stroking my clit, teasing and tormenting me. My brain numbed from the intense orgasm that started brewing inside. A broken cry escaped my throat from the fierce pressure building deep. I was quickly reaching the point of insanity as my fingers fisted the cushion over my head. I was close... oh, so close! His mouth continued the torture with a maddening drive.

My orgasm rippled through me, overwhelming in its intensity. A harsh moan ripped my throat. Seeing me unravel from his touch, his eyes turned wild. He wanted to possess me.

Gasping for air, I struggled to regain my composure and steady my breathing. Nick settled beside me on the chaise, gently brushing the disheveled strands of hair away from my face.

"Are you okay continuing with your birth control pills?" He pulled off his T-shirt and then his jeans and briefs.

I nodded, unable to form words.

"I want to be inside you. No more barriers, Ivy." His eyes bore into mine, a silent question of if I understood what he meant.

"That's how I like it too," I agreed, blushing. Still riding the remnant of the earlier orgasm.

"I want you." Turning on his side, he ground himself against my ass, proving the effect I had on him. On his body.

Nick got on top and slid all the way inside me, filling me up with a sweet ache. My earlier orgasm had left me relaxed, allowing him to move effortlessly. He set a leisurely rhythm. "Open your eyes for me. I want to see you when you savor this moment. Us."

I obliged, taking in his deep eyes and his beautiful face.

"I wish I could show you what I see in your eyes. How beautiful you truly are and how lucky I am." I couldn't talk, so he went on. "Your beauty, your brain, your wits—I'm under your spell. Even when you're angry, you take my breath away. I'm in awe of everything you are. I want to possess you, Ivy."

His lips grazed a sensitive spot behind my ear, and his warm breath on my neck drove me insane. Nipping, touching, kissing my hyper-sensitive skin all made the pressure brew inside my core once again. His back arched. I squeezed his ass with my hands as I braced myself for another mind-numbing orgasm.

Boxing me between his elbows, he raised himself until our eyes met again. He was not ready to break this contact, either. His eyes filled with hunger, gratitude, and something else that I couldn't quite understand; love, I assumed.

Nick's steady thrust and ragged breaths mirrored my own uneven rhythm. He seemed on the verge of speaking, holding back until the words finally broke free. "You feel so right.

Everything about this feels so good, baby. I want this more... again and again."

"I feel the same," I uttered.

"You'll always be mine." He reaffirmed his declaration. "I want to hear it, Ivy. From here on, it's only us."

"Yes, it's only us," I answered, breathing in his ardor.

He broke apart, filling me with his seed. Pleasure roared through me and I exploded around him as a powerful orgasm rippled from my core. My nails dug into his taut back, his grunts making me dizzy. Gripping him tightly, I milked every second of our combined pleasure. His husky growls filled my ears, driving me insane. We reached the pinnacle together as I climaxed around him.

His heartbeat synced with mine, his semi-hard erection nudging me from the inside. We waited to calm our breathing before we gave into our insatiable need again.

I had spent a lifetime waiting to be with Nick. Now that I had him right here on top of me, claiming me, the triumph erased old memories. I gave into him completely, over and over, until the need for sleep won over and I went out like a light in the safety of his arms.

Chapter Four

I enjoyed the quiet and his company. His arm possessively wrapped around my shoulder, making me feel safer than anywhere else I could have been. Even his high tower, hidden from the outside world, and even against the weight of my nightmares that didn't belong in our perfect bubble, nothing compared to the safety he provided. I traced his chiseled jawline, the hollows of his cheeks, his angled eyebrows, his long nose, and his sculpted lips. I had two words and two words only to describe him: *Greek god*.

Invariably, my fingers went back to the scar on his arm that started at his shoulder and went halfway to his elbow. An accident that happened when I was sixteen. It drew us closer, adding depth and dimensions to our ever-evolving relationship. Trust and faith and credence. A diminutive copy of the same scar on my ankle was the only piece of Nick I had carried with me.

"Did you ever think of getting rid of the scar?" I asked him.

He put his finger over mine and we traced it in unison. "I

can't even imagine that. It was the only fragment I had of you through all these years."

"That's exactly what I thought about my own scar," I whispered. My sentiments mimicked his words.

The bike accident had left me with a broken ankle, and Nick had been badly injured trying to save me. The twenty-four hours afterwards had been the most terrifying of my life as Nick drifted in and out of consciousness from blood loss. It had been made worse by him insisting on waiting for hours until my own surgery was complete when we were brought in and the doctors confirmed I wasn't in any danger.

"I'll never forget that night, Nick. I could have lost you forever." The lump in my throat didn't let me continue. The pain and horror of almost losing him were still etched in my mind, no different from the loss of my parents all those years ago. I hadn't been with Mom and Dad when I lost them. It felt like I hadn't had a choice either way. With Nick...there had been no way I could have let him go.

"The way you took care of me that night, watched over me..." Nick swallowed. "There was nothing in the world that could have kept us apart. Not even death."

"Yet you never tried to contact me when I left after our recovery." I was ruining the moment, but I couldn't hold back. Despite all the reasons he gave me and no matter how many times he reminded me of our ten-year age gap, I couldn't bring myself to forgive him for not contacting me all those years.

When I heard nothing, I craned my neck to meet his gaze. Those beautiful, vibrant green eyes glimmered through the tendrils of his hair, damp with sweat. "You realize I won't let you live it down, right?"

"Is that so?" His left eyebrow arched, and a smile played on the corner of his lips. "What must I do to earn your forgiveness?"

I broke free of his embrace and got off the chaise. As I started collecting our clothes that were strewn all around, Nick tried grabbing my hand. I was quick, and he failed.

"It's going to be hard." I feign a smirk, seizing the chance to suffuse him with guilt.

"Ivy!"

I stuck my tongue out at him and ran for the door. "Because I'm never going to forgive you."

Nick was quick to get to his feet and came after me. "Then I've got to *make* you forgive me."

Squealing, I ran into the living room, all the while trying to slip into my clothes. I only put on my panties when he caught up and wrapped his arms around my waist, pulling me back. We fell onto the couch together, laughing.

A wrestling match ensued. Getting on top, he pinned me on the couch while I batted my arms against his chest. He took full advantage of my nakedness, kissing every bit of my exposed skin. Quickly, he discovered my most sensitive spots, and he couldn't get enough of it.

"Okay, fine. I'll think about forgiving you!" I gasped, trying to talk between giggles.

He got up, taking me with him. "Think fast because it's dinner time, and I could devour you all night."

———

NICK PICKED UP TWO MARBLE DOMES AND THE aroma of herb-crusted lamb chops with mashed potatoes and asparagus filled the kitchen. I helped carry our warm plates to the table while Nick opened a bottle of Château Lafite Rothschild and poured it into two glasses. He slid one glass over to me and took the chair beside me.

I inhaled the spices—basil and herbs. "It smells delicious."

"Only the best for you."

I put my left hand on his thigh, not ready to break our contact just yet. Nick entwined his fingers with mine, leaving his left hand to eat.

"You're not left-handed," I noted.

He grinned at me. "Maybe I just don't want to let go of your hand."

My heart swelled.

"Do you eat at home?" I asked, hoping to calm my blushing face down from how much he wanted to remain connected to me.

"Rarely, if ever."

"Hmm..." I bit a piece of the lamb, which was cooked to perfection. "Sounds like we're very different people with very different lifestyles."

"Is that right? Give it a week. I'll mold you into mine."

I chuckled. "A man can always hope." Putting another piece of juicy meat into my mouth, I realized how famished I was after skipping breakfast and lunch.

"More like, *this man gets what he wants*." He pointed at his chest with the sharp end of the fork.

"I'm strong-willed. Don't you forget that."

"And I'm a man of many talents, persuasion being one of them. You can't deter me so easily."

I shrugged. "So be it. Don't say I didn't warn you."

"Warning noted. And dismissed."

He knew how to rile me up and sound hot at the same time. I needed to get off the topic before he truly riled me up more than he turned me on. "How was work? Are you done catching up?"

"Work is work." He sighed. "I looked forward to spending the evening with you."

There it was again, his million-watt smile I loved so much.

And it was as good a time as any to say what I had to say, so I did. "I'm sorry you had to miss work because of me. I wasn't expecting you to be looking for me when I left Saturday night after our argument."

His fork made a sound when it touched the plate. His gaze shifted to me with all seriousness. "Please don't run next time. If something bothers you, talk to me. Okay?"

I nodded. The distance and the agony in my heart sat like dread upon my chest. Only I knew how tormenting those forty-eight hours had been. The only good thing that came out was it gave me time to think and feel. My feelings for Nick superseded everything.

After re-connecting with Nick, I broke my two-year long relationship. Mike and I were never meant to be that much I knew from the beginning, but I kept trying while I was with him.

I was Nick's. I always was his.

With a kiss, I reinstated my promise before we went back to our dinner.

"About tomorrow..." Nick began. "Unfortunately, I have a dinner meeting I can't get out of. I hate the idea of you being at home all alone. Join me? I promise we'll do something fun after."

"That's what you usually do instead of eating at home?" I asked, wanting to understand his schedule.

"Mostly, yes. I will start freeing my evenings from now on, but tomorrow's dinner I can't get out of."

My heart leaped under my ribcage. He was changing his lifestyle to spend more time with me where I was running away questioning his intensions. "That's very considerate of you, but I already have plans."

He gave a sideways glance. "One day in the city and you already have plans, huh?"

"You probably don't remember, but I was supposed to be here the entire week. I'm actually running behind schedule. Dustin texted me when I was in Boston. We school friends are meeting for dinner."

Nick frowned, making me rethink of our conversation. "What's wrong?" I asked.

"I don't like Dustin." He turned gruff.

I tried not to laugh. "You don't even know him. Dustin and I have been friends since we were kids. Growing up, we were neighbors and our parents were friends. We even went to the same school." I elaborated on this, hoping to make him feel better. "He's nice and fun. Spend some time with him, I promise you'll change your mind about Dustin."

"I doubt that. When will you be free? We can meet after."

"I guess that depends on how the dinner goes. I haven't seen them in ages, so we have a lot of catching up to do. And Ryan is coming home on Friday. We can meet on Saturday, if that works for you." I swallowed my last remaining bite of meat and washed it down with some wine.

When he remained silent, I turned to look at him—only to find him glaring at me, pissed-off. "You're joking, right?"

"What do you mean?"

"This won't work, Ivy. Make time for us even when you get busy. You've no idea how packed my schedule is, but I'm still here. With you."

What am I missing?

"I'm having a hard time understanding the expectation here, Nick. Tomorrow I'm seeing my friends, like people do. Friday I'm spending the evening with Ryan and Risha. Now that I've moved back and got a job, I need to find an apartment, and do a million other things. I'll always make time for us, but I have to take care of these things and get settled first."

"So, you're saying your job, Ryan, apartment, and your friends come before me?"

Seriously, what has crawled up his ass?

"That's not what I said."

"Where exactly do I fit into your schedule?"

"Let's not turn this into an argument," I warned him. "This is all new to me. I had dated guys before, but I wouldn't be with them every day. We met when we both had free time. It was a healthy relationship for both—"

"To hell with your healthy relationships." With a grunt, Nick took my face between his hands and kissed me, hard. His hands moved inside my hair, mussing with determination. Every time I tried to talk, he rolled his tongue around mine and my words got caught between our tussling. I let him go deeper. He sucked on my tongue harder and longer, making me forget our conversation all together.

By the time our mindlessly crazy kiss ended, I was already sitting on his lap, drenched in his scent and reliving the entire experience in my mind again and again.

"Stay tonight." It wasn't a question.

A little disoriented after that mind-numbing kiss, I wondered if that was exactly what Nick wanted—to make me woozy, so I'd give into his demands. "I have to be at Gwen's office by eight."

He bent down and nipped the hollow of my throat. "I'll get you there on time."

I encircled my arms around his neck. "Getting me to do what you want... is that one of those special talents you were talking about?"

"You're a quick learner, Ivy McAlister," he said, and winked at the same time. "Let's move in together."

I halted right there, pretty sure I laughed too, but too

stunned to know what was going on with me at that moment. "You realize our relationship has lasted a grand total of two days, right?"

"Two days. Or two thousand days. What does it matter? It's right when it feels right. And everything between us feels more than perfect."

"It's too early, Nick. Sure, I was born in New York, but I haven't lived here as an adult. I have to figure out how I fit into this city. For that, I need to live on my own for a while."

He sighed, visibly exasperated. "Do you want us to be together, Ivy?"

Of course I did, but that wasn't the point. Mike and I had dated for two years before he even asked me to move in with him. The way I felt about Mike wasn't even a fraction of how I felt about Nick, but moving in together on the second day was definitely extreme.

Focus on the question he asked, Ivy. Do you want to be with him?

I nodded in response, and that calmed him a little.

"Then stop overthinking. Stop saying no to everything I propose. If I do the same, we wouldn't last another day."

Fine, he was right. We both needed to work on managing our egos and expectations without losing ourselves. Or each other.

"Moving in together is a big step"

"Moving to Manhattan was an even bigger step for you," he retorted.

"I haven't lived with anyone before." Abby didn't count because she was my roommate and best friend.

"It's you and me," he reminded me, visibly irritated because it alluded to the possibility of me moving in with Mike if Nick hadn't intervened. "Focus on the future, Ivy."

When I didn't respond, Nick spoke again. "We don't have to decide everything tonight. If you don't want to discuss it on day two, I'll try again on day three."

I cracked up, which was exactly what he wanted. He scooped me up in his arms and carried me through the hallway into his master bedroom. Like the rest of the house, Nick's bedroom was also enormous and so very masculine.

We walked inside the closet. He took one of his T-shirts out of his closet drawer and handed it to me. I took it out of his hand and looked around while he started changing in front of me. Oddly enough, his closet didn't feel like a museum. The well-organized wardrobe followed a monochromatic color scheme, yet it felt like a place that was used daily. Organized, but untidy. Habitable. Cozy.

By the time I had changed and meandered into his master bathroom, which had a clawfoot bathtub dominating one side and a standing shower stall on the other, I noticed a brand-new toothbrush waiting for me on the edge of the double vanity.

"Looks like someone is prepared for these unplanned sleepovers," I teased, while removing the toothbrush from its packaging.

"Let's move into someplace new," Nick suggested to my reflection in the mirror.

"I'm kidding." I shrugged and brushed my teeth.

Knowing he had brought other women into his bedroom didn't feel right. But then, he had spent the night in my bedroom in Boston where I had also been with Mike. It was unfair of me to make a big deal out of this. And since every topic we discussed eventually led to an argument or a disagreement, I didn't want to push it any further.

We'll share the bed he has already shared with other women...

Putting that weird, hollow feeling aside, I washed my face,

flossed my teeth and ran a comb through my hair. Nick was beside me the entire time, watching me in silence. I took my time braiding my hair. Whatever was in his mind couldn't take shape as coherent words. Maybe he had the same gnawing feelings I had.

On his California king bed, he pulled me close. I wrapped my arms around him to make him into my body pillow and our legs tangled together. It was hard to tell where I ended and where he began, and we stayed like that, talking for hours.

I savored these moments... learning one another, discussing what we liked and disliked, and talking about our past and present... it truly felt like a dream. A bale of fantasy, a fabric of reality—softened, brightened, and enveloped me in sensation, a warm cocoon shielding me from the nightmares of my past.

I HAD BURNED WITH A WILD RAGE WHEN NICK walked into his parents' house with a woman four years ago. That year, I had come prepared to confess my feelings for him. To tell him I wanted him. He was more than my brother's best friend and I wanted to be more than his best friend's sister.

Unfortunately for me, I never got the chance. He introduced Celine to everyone at the dinner table and called me Ryan's *little sister*. That was all I was to him.

Heartbroken and confused, I wrote a bogus note about some school assignment and left Nick's parents' home in the middle of the night.

Then I waited for him to get in touch with me. A call, a text, a visit—at that point I would've taken anything.

He did nothing.

Consumed by grief, I lived in a state of anger and sadness for months. Once I broke through the heavy haze, I tried to lock all the memories of him somewhere in the back of my mind and started dating other guys.

In the beginning, I compared everyone to Nick. He was an enigma and the only man who I knew could complete me. No matter how much I tried, he never left me. Not even for a day.

As time went on, I decided not to torture myself and resigned to my fate.

And then came Mike.

I met him during my junior year at Harvard. He was caring, polite, and respectful of my boundaries from the very first day. We never argued or fought. Mike always did whatever brought a smile to my face. There was no pressure, no expectations, and no rush to move things faster. I wasn't happy, but I wasn't sad, either. I learnt to live with contentment.

Last summer, when Ryan came over to Boston, I introduced him to Mike and that day Mike officially became my boyfriend. He always lifted my spirit, and he was always there when I needed him.

A few months ago, Abby announced that she and her boyfriend, Parker, were moving to California. When I heard that, I knew big changes were coming. I was right, because two weeks ago, Mike asked me if I wanted to move in with him. Logically, it made sense, so I agreed.

For the last year, my past had haunted me. It constantly reminded me how I left my old life and abandoned Ryan. I didn't understand the gnawing feeling, but I had this nagging itch to come home, as if something was waiting to be uncovered in New York.

I bought my ticket to revisit my old life the day Mike and I decided to move in together. A last-minute trip, where one day I told Ryan I was coming home, and by the end of the week I was getting off the plane. The whirlwind of events that followed resulted in me moving back to my hometown permanently, and—for the first time—into Nick's arms.

Had I been told a week ago that my life would change in a matter of days, I would've laughed it off. Not because I hadn't wanted those changes, but I had stopped believing in miracles.

But it had happened. The miracle had become my new reality now.

Chapter Five

The sky was inky black outside Nick's bedroom window. I turned my head, glancing at the wall clock in the dim night light. It was only five in the morning. My body clock was used to waking up at Harvard's time and if I had been in Boston, I would be on my daily run by now, haunting my usual trail. *But you aren't at Harvard or in Boston anymore.*

My body didn't crave a run. Instead, I draped Nick's arm over my chest and cozily snuggled into him. At last, I was home where I belonged. Nick stirred beside me and pulled me closer until his chest was pressed to my back.

With sleep no longer an option, I selfishly woke him up. "Nick. Are you awake?"

"Now I am," he purred into my hair.

"I can't sleep."

"I can tell."

I rolled over and faced him. I couldn't keep putting off asking the pressing question we had both been avoiding. He opened his eyes and, as always, gave me his full attention. "Tell me, sweetheart. What's keeping you awake?"

"How do you think Ryan will react if he finds out about us?"

"*When* he finds out about us," Nick corrected. "It's just a matter of time. I'll figure out how to break the news before he gets it from someone else."

"It shouldn't be a problem, right? You guys are best friends, after all."

"I'll handle it." His brows furrowed with contemplation, but he gave nothing more.

"What would be his problem, though?"

He waited a few heartbeats to collect his thoughts. "For starters, our age difference. I know he's going to freak out. Secondly, he's understandably protective of you. He still thinks of you as his baby sister."

"I was with Mike before, and he was okay with it."

"We all knew it wouldn't last." He tried not to smirk, but I saw it anyway.

I loved Ryan to death, but I was an adult now. Also, when didn't I make my own decisions since our parents' death? "Well, he'll have to get over our age gap."

"Can you leave this for me to handle?" Though he put it as a question, I knew he wasn't inviting me into a discussion or debate.

"I *am* seeing him tomorrow," I reminded him.

"Avoid discussing us. Give me a few days and I'll take care of it."

My mood soured. Moving closer, I hugged Nick with everything I had and hoped it would wash away the discomfort in my chest. It didn't. I had been too independent for too long. I always did what I wanted to do, never needing my brother's permission for my choices in life. But then again, I had never dated his best friend before, either.

"Don't overthink it. We'll cross that bridge when we get to it," Nick said.

"What if he's not okay with it? He's my only family."

"Don't think for a minute that I forget that. Ryan is like a brother to me as well. I would never come between you two. But I won't let him come between us, either. Let me explain things to Ryan." His determination made me see past our hurdle. I wanted to be with Nick, and I also wanted Ryan to be happy with my choice.

His lips pressed to my neck, stopping my mind from short-circuiting. His hand cupped my ass, pulling me into him. In a swift motion, the T-shirt I wore was out of our way. And before I realized it, I had lost my train of thought. Desire rushed through my veins.

"I could get used to waking up like this," I murmured, when I regained my ability to speak and my brain could articulate once more.

"That's the plan, sweetheart. I want you to crave me when I'm not around and be ready for me when we are together." His low voice in my ear only had me growing more aroused. "I want you in my bed every day—I want you to wake up to my cock sliding into you."

Nick's words sent stronger waves of desire through me. His kisses were catalysts—confessions, admissions, and declarations of intent that unraveled me to pieces. Our hands, mouths, and bodies communicated that could only be felt, not translated into words.

Every time he was deep inside me, we became two living beings merged into one. An overwhelming need enveloped me entirely. It was impossible to tell where I ended and he began.

There were only our shared heartbeats, the rhythm of our breath, and the warmth of our entwined bodies.

Lost in the depth of our connection, I submerged in a space we occupied together, an escape from reality where nothing else existed except the sheer intensity of our existence.

———

"Good morning."

The aromatic scent of freshly roasted coffee filled my senses and a gentle kiss brushed between my eyebrows. I inhaled Nick's scent, breathing in his cologne—bergamot and sage. It was far more tempting than the coffee.

Yawning, I opened my eyes. "I don't know when I fell asleep."

He hummed. "I couldn't bring myself to wake you sooner. I love to see you sleep in my arms. If I didn't have a meeting this morning, we'd still be in bed."

I tried to breathe in his scent again before I lifted my gaze to him properly. A charcoal suit and a black shirt were a nice contrast to his whitewashed skin and sandy brown hair. I reached for his white tie and pulled him down to me. "Good morning."

"Thank you for last night," Nick said between our playful kisses. Happiness and love poured out of his perfect smile. I couldn't help but mirror him.

He took the coffee mug from the nightstand and waited until I sat up before handing it to me. "And thank you for the kiss."

I sipped, willing myself to wake up. "I didn't take you for a man who knew how to make coffee."

He rolled his eyes. "Mrs. Martinez, my housekeeper. She's

in the kitchen now. She made it. But I know how to use a coffee maker." He lifted his chin to prove his point, as if that was some sort of achievement. "I hope I gave her the right instructions."

"Coffee is perfect. Exactly how I like it." I drank a few more quick sips before I got out of bed.

"I promised you'd be at work on time and I intend to keep my promise. I'll take you to Ryan's first, for you to change, and then I'm dropping you off at the university."

"You don't have to stick around after you drop me off at Ryan's. I'll take the subway."

"Like hell you will." He walked into his closet and came back with a pair of silver cufflinks. "But I agree. We work on opposite sides of the city. I need to get you a car so it can be at your disposal."

My outburst of laughter turned his head back to me. I couldn't with that whole notion. "There's no way I will accept that, Nick. I live in the city and I'll use the subway like every other New Yorker."

In a moment's time, his playful eyes turned grave. "This topic is not up for discussion. Get ready. I don't want you to be late." He nudged me toward the bathroom before he started working on his cufflink again.

"I was deciding not to argue with you anymore, but you don't make things easy, do you?"

He smirked, but stayed silent.

"Let's add this to our list of the many things we have to discuss," I told him curtly, as I left him and walked inside the shower. And just so he was certain I meant it, I called loudly, "It's an absolute *no!*"

———

INSIDE NICK'S PRIVATE ELEVATOR, HE PRESSED THE button for the basement level garage and entered his keycard into the slot. Taking a step towards me, he captured a partially damp lock of my hair and coiled it between his fingers.

"My shirt looks better on you." His eyes scanned me, taking in his white shirt that I wore, making me acutely aware of how little I wore underneath. No bra, his briefs only. His lips brushed mine. Once. Twice. He took my bottom lip, sucking and nipping, driving me insane.

"You insatiable monster," I laughed, hoisting myself up on my toes to match his demands, all the while pulling down the shirt to make sure it covered my thighs. "You better get me to Ryan's apartment before someone sees me like this, or it'll be our last day together."

Public nudity was never my thing, but I was also a completely different person with Nick. I wasn't hiding anymore. I was thriving, fully and unapologetically myself.

He removed his jacket and draped it over my shoulders. The jacket didn't cover much, except his guilt over ripping my dress and lacy undergarments half an hour ago when he'd craved me once again, when I'd been fresh out of the shower and dressed, as if he needed more to get him through the day.

"I'll make sure no one sees you like this except me."

"I don't care. They can see me, but they can't have me."

He growled in approval, but then he changed his mind and said, "I care. That *I've just been thoroughly fucked* look on your face is meant only for me."

The floor shook slightly when the elevator door started to open behind me. Suddenly, Nick looked up and the expression on his face turned from a smile to confusion to fury.

I turned, trying to see what caught his attention, and my breath hitched.

Nick tugged me behind him so the men standing before us wouldn't see me in nothing but his shirt and jacket. I noticed Tom, Nick's driver and bodyguard, along with a few other men. As soon as they caught sight of me, they immediately averted their eyes.

"We're taking the Navigator today," Nick announced, shielding me from the men.

As we walked, I noticed every parking spot had 'Reserved for Nicholas Branson' signs on the wall. We were in Nick's private garage section, with at least five men in dark suits roaming around. And finally, I saw what everyone was inspecting.

"Did something happen to your Lamborghini?" I asked Nick, once the initial shock of running into others while I was in such a state wore off.

"Car thieves happened." He opened the back passenger door of the black SUV for me and waited as I climbed in. Then he leaned down and said, "Give me five minutes to deal with this. I'll be right back."

I bobbed my head, equal parts curious and shocked.

Through the tinted window, I assessed the damage ahead. The brutally slashed tires of his bright yellow Lamborghini stood out. The same car Nick used over the weekend to take me to his parents' house. The only logical explanation was when the thieves couldn't steal his car, they damaged it out of spite.

Nick paced the garage in a fury, shouting into his phone. John, the man who had dropped me off at Ryan's apartment the day before, went around the garage looking for clues to solve the mystery. Tom and the rest of the men were checking other cars to see what other damage had been done.

Fifteen minutes later, Nick got into the car and settled beside me. "Don't worry. Everything is okay."

"It's your favorite car," I said in complete disbelief.

"Yes. It was." A vein in his temple throbbed. Nick was pissed.

"There are so many cars here. Clearly, you're a collector. Why did they go for this particular one?"

"It's not just any car. This is an Aventador SVJ Coupe."

I gave him a puzzled look. He threw his head back and laughed. "It's one of a kind."

"Of course it is." I rolled my eyes. They all seemed exclusive brands that you don't see on the road every day. "Any idea who the thief was?"

"My security team is looking into it."

The same security team that went looking for me when I left Manhattan last weekend? The team that searched every road and train station from here to Boston for forty-eight hours while I was cooped up in Abby's home in Marlborough, Massachusetts?

I tried to understand the depth of the situation. "Has this happened before?"

"This is New York for you," Nick said vaguely. His ticking nerves gave it away, though. He was feigning calm. "I'll make sure it never happens again."

"What can you possibly do to stop this? It isn't something you can control."

"I'll find a way. Don't regret moving back, Ivy." Nick kissed my forehead and turned to Tom, who was already in the driver's seat. "Let's go to Ryan's for Ivy to change before we're both late for work." Then he turned his attention to me again and said, "You need to move your stuff out of Ryan's place. This isn't practical."

———

Buttoning Nick's jacket over his dress-shirt, I walked up the McAlister building's elevator with confidence. I tried to get over the unease that was still lingering in my chest. More than the car, Nick was concerned about my apprehension. It took me the entire ride to convince him I would not leave him or New York because of the incident with his car. I was here to stay.

I slipped into a green pencil dress. Almost half of my clothes were of that color. Consciously or subconsciously, I picked emerald shades whenever I went shopping. Nick's eyes kept me captivated even when we hadn't met in years.

Next, I dried my hair and put it in a high ponytail. I was going with classy and professional, but memorable. As memorable as my first day working for Gwen was going to be, I didn't think it would involve attempted car theft, that was all.

I returned to Nick and the SUV in less than ten minutes, which had to be some sort of record. As Tom drove the car through the city streets, a typical New York morning started unfolding before me. Traffic getting worse by the minute, pedestrians filling up every crossing, and cab drivers honking for no particular reason. There was more graffiti on buildings than I remembered and I spotted quite a few homeless people, too.

This city was nothing but a melting pot of the best and worst things, and you never knew what you were going to get on any day. I was happy to be part of it all again. Not as a tourist, or a traveler, but as a resident.

Nick had been on his Bluetooth since we left Ryan's. He was handling business, of course. A big audit meeting was happening tonight, and Nick wanted to review everything beforehand.

"*Control freak* should be your middle name," I muttered under my breath, recalling his little joke from last night.

Throughout the drive and his call, his hand never left mine, conveying silent reassurance—security and comfort—promising that everything would be okay. Despite the distraction and demand of the phone conversation, that simple gesture spoke volumes about the depth of our connection.

I would've given anything to see him in action, dominating a room full of executives. . It was another one of my fantasies because I'd only ever interned at startups. I had no plans to join the corporate world yet; but then, I hadn't decided what I wanted to do after my MBA, either. Since my parents' death, I had only ever planned one step at a time.

At ten minutes to eight, we reached the red brick building where Gwen's office was located. As soon as the car stopped, Nick switched off his Bluetooth and gave me his full attention. Tom got out of the car and gave us privacy.

"Don't say no," Nick told me. "Stay with me tonight."

I couldn't stop smiling. "Yes, I'd love that."

Sliding his hand behind my back, he brought me closer. His other hand held my chin, pulling my face up to meet his. His biceps flexed under the palm of my hand, my chest heaving against his, as if, whenever we were close, our bodies automatically wanted to be in sync.

Our relationship was new, and I was still discovering various facets of Nick. This one I adored—butterflies and hearts. This version of him made me feel like the luckiest girl in the world.

Reluctantly, he let go of me, leaving me panting. "I'll pick you up after dinner." He didn't ask.

I shook my head, still reeling from our kiss. His tongue slid inside my mouth, catching me off guard. His hand cupped my breast, pushing and pulling, kneading one at a time. My nipples pebbled at the stimulation. Heat pooled between my legs. *Shit*. He was playing dirty.

"You're not playing fair," I breathed.

"You're a quick learner, Miss Smartass. Now go or you'll be late."

The exterior red bricks of the university building glowed under the morning sun. Excitement and nerves brewed inside, leaving me buzzing with a fresh wave of energy. As I walked, the distant hum and chatter of students filled my ears. I smiled at everyone who passed me and said hello to everyone who looked my way. I might've left Boston, but Boston hadn't left me. It had taught me to be the friendliest person in a busy crowd.

I entered Gwen's room after knocking once. Today, there was another desk opposite hers.

"It will be easier for us to collaborate this way." She showed me to my new office desk, which was an exact replica of hers.

I walked around the room which wasn't fancy—stark white walls with one large glass pane window to the left of my desk overlooking the street below. I pulled the bottom drawer and dropped my bag after removing the laptop.

"This room can do with a bit of sprucing up," she said. "Personalize your desk if you like."

"Thanks, I've never done that before." I'd been a private

person for far too long. Even during my previous internships, I had kept my privacy intact. No one associated Ivy McAlister with *the McAlister Group*.

She nodded. Without asking for further details, she returned to her workstation and turned the screen so I could see. "I also keep my private and professional life separate, though at times it's hard to separate one from the other. Our individuality is shaped by our surroundings, professionally or otherwise."

Gwen was right, but a big part of me hoped to keep my private life private. Her focus returned to her screen. I walked over to her desk and joined her. "I have three parallel projects running. One is a technology company based out of Vegas that's almost at the finishing stage. One is Blue Chip Corporation, where you interned in your senior year. By the way, your work was impressive."

"Thanks," taking compliments wasn't something I was comfortable with either. "I didn't know you were also involved with Blue Chip."

"You single-handedly fixed their finance and human resource issues by bringing those departments in-house and shred unnecessary overhead increasing profitability by fifty percent in a matter of a year. I'm sure you had your hands full," she responded with a smile, making me curl under the weight of acclaim.

"Blue Clip was a good team and they were open to my suggestions. They made everything easier," I had to be honest because they were really great, unlike some of my classmates who had tough clients and uphill battle at every stage.

"You really don't know how to take compliments, do you?" I was sure my face turned a different shade as she continued, "You were brilliant. I consulted directly with the executives that's why you and I never crossed paths. And really, I never had to work because you came up with every solution on your own. I want you to take over Indy Corp. They are much larger than Blue Chip and into clean energy who needs to reduce their expenditure considerably and start showing profits in the next three to six months, but they have very thin margins to work with, so completely unique challenges."

"I'm looking forward to new challenges," I said eagerly. For a nerd like me, there was no better way to spend the summer.

Business development for startups was what I specialized in. It was also the reason I had decided not to join the McAlister Group; I wanted to concentrate on small businesses and help increase their productivity and profitability. Hence, this opportunity to work with Gwen was a dream come true.

After talking for the next two hours, Gwen asked me to start with some market research. Thankfully, Indy had a great online presence, so I had a lot to work with. My nerdy brain had found its oxygen.

In the afternoon, Gwen told me she had lunch plans with faculty members and stepped out. I wanted a change of scenery too, so I made a quick trip to the cafeteria to grab a sandwich. I had no plans to eat there, though.

While waiting in line to pay, I checked my phone. A message from *Love* was at the very top. Before I opened it, I switched over to my contacts and changed the name from *Love* to *Nick*.

Miss you already. How's your first day going so far? Not ignoring you, it's been a busy day today.

Instead of texting him back, I called him.

"Ivy!" Nick's voice tucked itself into my heart. Immediately, I smiled. "I was just telling the guys I'm the luckiest man alive."

"Who are these guys?"

"My staff," he answered. "You should come over and meet them."

"Mr. Branson, I'm a working woman now," I said, laughing, and moved with the lunch line.

"My Miss Independent. I hoped to pursue you to join Branson Capital."

"And do what? Act as your sexy secretary?"

"Hmm. That evokes many ideas," Nick chuckled. "Something worth discussing tonight. Coming to the point though, at the meeting, everybody was asking why I was in such a good mood. The answer came naturally: it's you."

"What an interesting conversation for a meeting." I grabbed the opportunity and asked what was on my mind. "Does that mean we're exclusive now?"

"Where did that come from?" he said without a beat.

"Forget I asked. I don't even know why I said that." Embarrassed, I wanted to hide under a rock. But it was too late to retract my question.

What am I thinking? We just started dating.

"Sweetheart, I thought I made myself very clear. You and I are both off the market."

Permanently? I stopped from going ahead of myself. "Thanks for clarifying."

"I don't share what's mine. And you are completely, irrevocably mine."

"And the other way around?" I immediately challenged.

"Goes without saying. We're together now. That's why you should move in with me."

"Nick, it's too fast. We don't know if we can survive without killing each other." Another payment counter opened, and the line moved faster. I moved with it.

"I know everything I need to know. If you have questions, just ask. With you, I'm an open book."

"Okay." I cleared my throat. "For starters, I don't even know how many girlfriends you had until now."

He responded in a heartbeat. "We both had our share of partners. We shouldn't let our pasts dictate our future, Ivy. From here on out, it's only you and me. You are my future. Isn't that enough?"

He knocked the air out of me without even trying. "It's more than enough," I whispered, still reeling. "We still need time to get to know one another."

"And we will. It's still not a good enough reason to live separately, though. I've waited too long to not have you this close, Ivy."

"Same." My face flushed. I looked at my surroundings, and thankfully, no one was watching me.

"Good. So, you are moving in?"

"Not so fast, mister." As much as I wanted the same thing as Nick, I couldn't jump into another major decision of my life. Deciding to change the course of our discussion, I asked, "any news on the thieves?"

"My team is still investigating." His voice turned gruff, either from the change of topic or because he wasn't over what had happened to his car this morning.

"Are you okay?" I asked when he didn't talk for the next couple of seconds. The weight of his morning fury weighed heavily on my shoulders.

"No. I won't be able to drive my favorite car until they send a replacement."

He sulked like a little child. I shook my head, trying not to make fun of his feelings. Men and their toys.

"Hold on," he said abruptly. I heard some muffled voices in the background before he spoke again. "I've got to go. My dinner will end by nine. Can I pick you up at nine-thirty?"

I reached the counter to pay for my sandwich. "That should work. See you later, babe."

By the time we hung up, another message was waiting for me. It came from Dustin.

All set for tonight? Happy Hour @ 5:00, Victoria Hotel and Bar. It's near the house. Btw, technically we're not neighbors anymore. I live near Columbia.

I handed my credit card to the cashier and typed out a response. **That works. Thanks for telling me you moved before I knocked on your penthouse door and scared some stranger.**

Dustin responded right away, bringing a smile to my face. ***My parents still live there. They're in Europe on holiday right now, but they would love to see you when they get back.***

The possibility of seeing Pauline and William after so many years filled me with nostalgia. **I would love that. Looking forward to their return.**

I dropped my phone back into my purse, took my lunch, and headed back to my desk.

———

"Is this Gwen Sinclair's office?"

I looked up from my laptop screen to find a gorgeous man standing in the doorway.

What was it with New York and hot men?

I put my sandwich back on the plate and wiped my lips with a napkin. "She just stepped out. Can I help you with something?"

"Bummer! I was hoping to catch her before I left. Then again, I should've probably called her first." He came inside the room and extended his hand. "Damien Westford. And you are?"

Lean but muscular, sandy hair, green eyes, and sculpted facial features—this man had everything going for him except for being in the wrong city. I could see him somewhere in Malibu, working in a Hollywood movie. Maybe he was part of a television show in Manhattan itself? Based on his tailored suit, it was evident he came from money. Women must fall for him all the time.

"Ivy McAlister. I'm assisting Professor Sinclair." I took his hand. He gave a firm handshake before releasing it.

"I didn't know Gwen hired someone."

"It's my first day," I clarified. "She'll be back soon if you want to wait for her. Or you can email her, I guess. Sorry, I'm not sure what the protocol is."

"I'll do that. If Gwen hired you, you must be good. She's too picky." He leaned against Gwen's desk, folded his arms, and got comfortable. His smile reached his eyes, twinkling with something mischievous, and his full attention remained on me.

His charm instantly put me at ease. I was pretty sure I wasn't the only one to fall under his spell. "I would also be totally full of myself if I say that's the case."

"Humble and smart. How did we not meet earlier? Usually, I'm the one who hires interns and there is no way I would've seen you and not remembered."

Was he flirting with me?

"That's because I recently moved back from Boston." Now that I said it out loud, it sounded too real. "I did my undergrad there."

"Don't tell me... Harvard?"

I tilted my head in disbelief. "What gave it away?"

"It was a wild guess, but I was ready to bet my money on it."

We both laughed. I found him easy to talk to.

"If you're ever looking for an internship, let me know. We're always searching for new recruits."

"I'm not sure what your company does, but for now, I'm happy with the job I have."

"Our focus is on client's asset management. Think about it."

From his wallet, he removed a metallic business card and handed it to me. "I own Imperial Portfolio Management," he stated with a hint of pride, even though the card clearly said President. "I'll get going now, unless you'd like to grab a coffee."

Smooth.

I pointed at my laptop. "Sorry, I'm on the clock. Maybe some other time."

Diplomatic and subtle. Internally, I thanked my mentor Abby for teaching me all the tricks to avoid men without being impolite.

"Absolutely." He gave me an unmistakably flirty smile. "It was a real pleasure meeting you."

"Same here. I'll let Gwen know you stopped by."

"No need. We're meeting tomorrow. I hope to see you soon, too." He left waving goodbye. I again resumed my work.

———

I DIDN'T REALIZE THE WORKDAY HAD ENDED UNTIL Gwen got up from her desk. "You don't have to finish everything today," she said. "I finish work around three, but you can build a schedule that works for you."

"Three works for me as well," I told her, with a quick exhale. I had been staring at my monitor for the last two hours straight. Other than a brief hello when Gwen returned, I hadn't really spoken to her since my lunch.

"This is all very exciting. Challenging, but exciting. I need to do more research and figure out how the company can cut costs without compromising the quality. Their biggest challenge is the cost of raw materials. Buying them locally is turning out to be too expensive and is eating into their profit margin. I get it though, the goal of this company is to lower their carbon footprint and that comes with a cost." I explained after spending the day understanding Indy Corp.

"Be creative, Ivy. I say look at other countries that export similar products," Gwen said.

"I've got another plan, why import when we have quality manufacturers right here? Have you heard of the 3-D printing company that's slowly making waves?" When she stopped unplugging her laptop and looked at me, I knew I had grabbed her attention. "Another startup out of New Jersey. They're small right now, but they have the potential to grow big."

"Interesting," she remarked, trying to see where I was going with that.

"Introduce two small companies and let them both grow together by helping each other out," I continued. "This printing company has brought large 3-D printers from Europe and is asking US customers to try them out."

"What an excellent idea. But helping another company? What's in it for us?" She waited for my answer.

"We work with them today, they know who to call when they need advice."

"And if they don't need advice?"

Gwen was definitely testing me. I was a novice, she was a master—but I took a stab at answering, anyway. "They all need advice if they want to grow their business. Otherwise, they'll become stagnant with no future."

She gave me an approving smile and got on with unplugging her laptop. "You got it. And don't think I don't trust your business instincts. It would surprise you how many students forget the basics. Anyway, enough about work. Don't forget to have some fun as well. It is your summer vacation after all. Any plans for tonight?"

I switched off my laptop, getting up from my seat. "I'm meeting some old school friends for dinner."

"Sounds fun! Should we walk to the subway station together?"

"Sure." I slid my laptop inside the bag and followed her out.

Gwen and I soon realized we had a lot in common. We talked about the university cafeteria and about the coffee shops around Harvard. Guilt washed over me once again. I couldn't believe that in less than a week, I'd made such a big decision about my life and left my safety bubble behind.

We crossed the lobby. I pushed through the building door and the heatwave engulfed us.

"Have you ever lived in New York before?" I asked Gwen.

"My first husband and I spent many years here before I moved to Boston. I enjoyed my time in the city, but—"

"Miss McAlister!"

Gwen's sentence was left unfinished when we were interrupted by someone calling my name. Simultaneously, we both turned to see John standing on the curb. Not sure how I hadn't noticed him when we exited the building.

In his gray suit and dark shades, the guy was a shorter version of the Terminator. "Miss McAlister, Mr. Branson has sent the car for you."

He stood beside a sleek black SUV Audi. Embarrassed, I tried to conceal my irritation. "Please tell Mr. Branson I am taking the subway home."

"I would advice against it, Miss McAlister." Apparently, John was persistent.

Unfortunately for him, so was I. He could intimidate people around him, but I held my ground. "I didn't agree to the car, Mr. Branson should know."

Gwen looked at us for over a minute. "All right, Ivy," she intercepted. "I'll see you tomorrow morning."

To avoid making an even bigger scene, I said goodbye to Gwen and got into the SUV.

"Ryan's apartment, please," I instructed.

Even the scent of the brand-new car had no effect on my anger. Nick had once again interfered in my personal life after I told him not to. My phone rang nonstop throughout the ride, but I doubted anything good would come out of answering it. Knowing this had to be dealt with in person, I ignored my phone with no remorse.

The SUV stopped outside the building. I thanked John, my chauffeur, though with his thick build, tanned skin, short hair, and black sunglasses, he looked more like a bodyguard.

I unbuckled my seatbelt, ready to get out, when John's voice made me pause. "Can you please check your phone, Miss McAlister? Mr. Branson is trying to reach you."

"Please, call me Ivy. And thank you again for the ride."

I got out of the big black car and slammed the door shut. I had to get some things straightened out right away.

Chapter Seven

An hour-long shower couldn't alleviate my mood. When I switched off the faucet, hot steam lingered, just like the endless things stacked up to *discuss later* with Nick. It was all I had been saying to myself. *We'll talk about it later.* I forced myself to compartmentalize different aspects of my life. My goal was to have a good time with my friends instead of sulking. The impending discussion with Nick was bound to be serious. But I refused to let my sour mood ruin a perfect evening.

As soon as I exited through the main entrance, I spotted the SUV waiting outside. I turned the other way and mixed into a random group of pedestrians. Making sure I wasn't followed, I walked the last four blocks to my destination with ease. The upbeat crowd crawled with me and allowed me to feel the pulse of Manhattan.

It also helped me forget what was coming later that night. Another argument.

I was walking into the Hotel Victoria when my phone pinged. Annoyed, I took it out of my purse with every intent to switch it off completely when I realized the message was from Ryan.

Now, that I can't ignore.

I will be home by noon tomorrow. Looking forward to spending time with you.

I sent a quick text telling him I missed him and looked forward to seeing him as well. Putting my phone back in my purse, I walked inside.

Art nouveau to the core, the Hotel Victoria had a distinct style. With its blue mosaic-tiled floors and blue-and-gold accent walls, the place was the perfect mix of hip and sophistication. Abby would've called it *'Insta-worthy'*, happily devoting hours to taking pictures of every fascinating part of the lobby.

Signs pointed to all the restaurants on the second floor. I followed their direction. When I entered the Bar and Grill restaurant, the retro style one of three restaurants of this hotel, a woman with a very prominent heart-shaped face, full lips, and curly blonde hair started running toward me. Imitating her, I did the same. We were full of smiles. When we met somewhere in the middle, I pulled her into a tight hug. A good few inches shorter than me, even in high heels, she hadn't changed one bit.

"Rachael! You have no idea how much I missed you." Unable to hold back, I pulled her into an embrace for the second time.

"Not more than I missed you. You literally vanished off the face of the earth!" She complained.

Back in the day, we were inseparable. That was until my life took a full one-hundred-eighty-degree turn and I distanced myself from everyone, including her. My closest friend all those years ago, she tried hard to break that wall. I made it impossible. Once I left New York, I did not stay in touch with anyone. Now, all these years later, I felt silly for pushing away the friends that people would've killed to have.

Noah and Dustin joined us soon after. A charming kid who had turned into a good-looking man, Noah was slightly shorter than me only because I was wearing heels. Whatever he lacked in the height department, he compensated for with extraordinary wit. And then there was Dustin, the fun one, who towered over all of us with striking sapphire blue eyes and a head full of curly black hair. I had always liked his easy-going personality. The four of us had been friends since preschool and we probably would've stayed friends if I hadn't run off to Boston.

We took refuge in one corner of the bar until our table was available. Our first drinks of the evening were ordered, and we picked up right where we had left off.

"Just finished my undergrad from Fashion Institute. Dad is financing my boutique in SoHo," Rachael enthusiastically updated me. "He'd rather I stay put than explore other areas."

"What can I say? He's a smart father and businessman," I quipped, and turned to Noah. "What're you up to?"

"I joined Dad's trading business. Now that I think of it, I should've waited a few months." Noah laughed. "But it's too late. He looks forward to seeing me in the office every day."

We had been kids who talked about fantasies and dreams, and here we were, talking about the real world. Business and work. I couldn't help but wonder where the time had gone.

"We might see each other more often since I've transferred to Columbia," I told them, mostly aiming my announcement at Dustin, who was a business student at Columbia I'd found that out when I met him last Friday at Hotel MoxTo's inauguration party. A joint venture between Ryan, Nick and their friend Taber, it was one of many hotels they owned together.

The cheers and squeals that followed started turning heads. We were too happy in our own little world—eight years of stories, both cringeworthy and happy, our successes and struggles, just waiting to be shared. One evening wouldn't be enough. But now that I was back, I had all the time in the world to share everything with my friends.

"I can't believe we're all together again. We missed you, Ivy," Noah said, as we clinked shot glasses.

"Same. And I'm really sorry about how I acted back then. I didn't handle things well."

"Nobody blames you for that." Dustin wrapped his arms around my shoulder for a comforting hug.

Rachael nodded in agreement. "You went through something terrible. Who knows how any of us would've acted if we were in your shoes?"

"Still, I feel terrible for not staying in touch."

"We forgive you. But remember, now you've got no excuse." Everybody agreed with Dustin, including me. "And don't change your phone number." Fine, I deserved that scolding, too.

I wasn't that person anymore. Dr. Patrick, my therapist, had spent years making sure I came out of my shell and got back to who I used to be. Being with Nick, returning to New York, catching up with old friends and restarting our friendship—this was my new beginning, a brand new chapter of my life.

"Are you staying with Ryan?" Rachael asked, pulling me out of my thoughts.

"For now, yes. But I'm going to look at other options soon. I can't live with my brother and his fiancée forever."

"I'm looking for a new apartment myself. You remember how we always said when we grew up, we'd share an apartment for a year?" Rachael reminded me of our conversation from a lifetime ago. When Ryan and Nick took an apartment during their junior year, Rachael and I made plans of our own. Who would've thought how our lives would turn out? "Well, what do you think?"

As tempting as that sounded, Nick had asked me to move in with him. I hadn't given him a definitive answer, but I had to. Soon. I wanted to walk with him, to breeze through each day and savor every moment. Instead, he wanted me to fly with him. My list of things to discuss with him was growing by the hour.

"Let me get back to you on that." I told her, finally.

"Take your time. I'm not in a rush," she said, then excitedly clapped her hands. "I still can't get over the fact that we're living in the same city again."

Dustin cleared his throat. "Same city? Ivy and I are going to be in the same class. Beat that, Rach!"

Already excited about Columbia, it dawned on me that Dustin and I would be together for the next two years. Growing up, he had been nothing but sweet and caring. Not only that, but our parents were friends, and we had all been neighbors for years. We'd spent years together, as well as with each other's families.

After an hour of catching up and spending time at the bar, the hostess took us to our table. Rachael and I shared a bright blue loveseat and Noah sat opposite us. Dustin took the wingback chair next to me. Any reservations I'd had before meeting them were long gone. We chatted non-stop.

"Aside from Columbia, any reason for moving back, Ivy?" asked Dustin, as the server placed the main courses in front of us. He watched me intently, clearly waiting for an unfeigned explanation.

"Honestly, I missed home. And I was ready to see what the city has to offer. The rest fell into place."

"I'm so happy you're back," Rachael exclaimed from beside me. "We have a lot of catching up to do and one dinner won't cut it." Showing off her chopstick skills, she fished out a piece of spicy tuna from her poke bowl.

"Goes without saying, Rach," I added while getting a stab on my bibimbap.

My jaw hurting from our incessant laughter, I couldn't be more excited about reconnecting with my Trinity friends. Our stories flowed effortlessly. Dustin was outright hilarious with his incredible memory. He kept us entertained with elementary school stories that we all had forgotten. Wherever Dustin's memory faltered, Noah seamlessly picked up the slack and filled in the missing details.

I was having the time of my life. Frankly, I couldn't remember the last time I laughed so much with these guys and felt so happy and light. It must've been before the devastating loss of my parents, which now felt like a distant memory from ages ago.

I was so busy chatting that it took me a while to notice an uninvited guest, who stood stoically behind the chair where Noah was seated. His unwavering gaze was fixed directly on me.

Chapter Eight

I glanced at the watch on my wrist and noticed it was only eight o'clock. My gaze shifted back to Nick, a mix of irritation and disbelief filling me. I never told him where I was, and yet he somehow found me. Gradually, the laughter around us died down when everyone realized I had stopped laughing. Confusion colored their faces.

Dustin was the first to rise from his seat and made his way towards Nick. "Hey man, good to see you."

They had met before, at MoxTo's opening. Nick shook Dustin's hand, but his eyes remained locked with me. "If you are done, we can go home now."

What? The? Fuck?

Completely embarrassed, I struggled to find an appropriate response. Outright barging in and telling me we had to leave? Even Ryan wouldn't have dared to pull a stunt like that. But I wanted to avoid a scene in front of my friends and I was too upset to label our relationship. I compromised. "Everyone, this is Nick."

"*Nicholas* Branson," he corrected.

The Prick, I should have added.

Noah seemed to know Nick well since they were in the same sort of business, but Nick didn't even try to have a semi-decent conversation with him. His mask in public was on, and he would not let anyone see beyond his hard, cold exterior. Right now, he was being downright rude. A self-absorbed jerk.

"I'm so sorry. There's somewhere we need to be, and it completely slipped my mind," I stammered, fumbling for an excuse.

Rachael took my hand. "I'll be near the university tomorrow. Let's meet for lunch? Around noon?"

"I would love that." I immediately agreed.

My blood bubbling inside, but I remained calm on the outside. With a cheerful face to show I was in control of the situation, I picked up my purse and headed outside without waiting for Nick. He had embarrassed me again. If that continued, I wasn't sure how long we'd last.

———

I took the stairs instead of the elevator. Down in the lobby, I walked out through the revolving door, turned right, and hit the sidewalk toward Ryan's apartment. Fury blinded me. I had learned how to control my fiery rage in therapy, but I struggled to remember the methods Dr. Patrick had taught.

The traffic light turned green. I stopped at the curb alongside the rest of the pedestrians, focusing on my breathing. *Deep inhale, exhale, inhale, exhale. See? The old trick still works.*

"Where the hell are you going?" Nick rushed up from behind and held my elbow.

A little buzzed and extremely furious, I nearly fell on him. "Leave me alone," I sneered, trying to be discreet among the crowd. "Haven't you embarrassed me enough?" Tears filled my eyes, ready to push over, a sign of weakness I didn't want to show.

The man beside me stole a quick glance in our direction. Nick's grip tightened and his face tensed, yet his gaze softened when he locked eyes with me once more. "Let's go home and talk about it."

"I'm not going anywhere with you," I seethed through gritted teeth.

"Either we go home and talk in private, or we do it here. Your choice." His tone shifted immediately like he was on the edge.

Taken aback by his stern voice and lack of regard for the surroundings, I just stared at him, dumbstruck.

Seconds felt like hours. The pedestrian crossed the street and a new set of pedestrians joined us. Nick waited for me to make a decision. I knew this wouldn't end until I went with him, but I wasn't ready to give in without a fight. "I don't want to go with you."

"That option is not on the table, Ivy."

"Who the hell are you to give me options?" Tonight, neither of us were ready to back down.

Nick's face contorted in frustration. "Will you stop acting like a brat and get in the freaking car?" Right on cue, his SUV pulled up in front of us.

Not wanting to attract any more curious eyes, I slid into the backseat. He followed and closed the door with a loud thud. The car weaved through the traffic, slowing down at Nick's building. The drive was too short to sort the weight of emotions I was carrying with me. Frustration simmering, a rage surging within me. I needed more time to calm down. The anger was still coursing through my veins and the anguish formed a lump in my throat. He was wrong on so many levels, yet he carried himself as if I was at fault.

As soon as the car came to a complete stop, I threw open the car's door. The doorman opened the building door even before I reached it. I stomped through the lobby toward the elevator. Nick followed at his usual pace, which somehow infuriated me further since I couldn't go up without his freaking keycard. Blood thumping through my ears, I was ready to explode—yet I waited.

The elevator rose slower than it did yesterday. The air was filled with palpable negativity and simmering exasperation, as if the air itself had turned acrimonious. Leaning against the cool mirrored wall behind me, I tried to calm down. It didn't help. As soon as the door opened, I headed through the foyer into the kitchen without breaking my stride. My eyes and ears burned with fury.

Nick had an uncanny ability to rile me up in the worst ways. To get under my skin and bring out the worst in me. I couldn't remember the last time I had felt this angry.

How could you forget, Ivy? It was exactly two days ago when he acted like a total douche in front of Mike.

"Ivy, wait," Nick commanded from the foyer. "Come back."

Desperate for some distance, I ignored him. In the kitchen, I poured and gulped down a glass of water, then filled it again. I wasn't thirsty, but I needed time to rein in my anger. The water didn't help. The distance, however, helped marginally. I went to the living room and sat down on the couch.

Nick watched me from the foyer in silence. After finishing the rest of the water, I put the empty glass on the center table and finally gathered enough strength to look at him. The vein in his temple pulsed. His face was flushed. Clearly, we were two peas in the same pod.

"Say what you have to say," I managed.

"Did you check my messages?"

"No."

"Why not?"

"Maybe because I didn't want to, Nick," I snapped. My anger made it hard to sit still, let alone speak. "Oh, yes. Now I remember. Without checking with me first, you sent a *freaking chauffeur* to pick me up after work!"

My outburst shocked us both. I was a grown woman. I had never lost control like that before.

"And it's a problem because?" he asked, keeping his temper in check. Clearly, he was doing a better job than me.

"Do you really not get it? I already told you I was going to take the subway. I was about to go there with Gwen. It was embarrassing."

"Why was it embarrassing? I don't want you to travel by subway."

"Sorry if I didn't make this clear before, but I don't like being controlled. *I* can decide how *I* want to travel!" My voice rose into a scream, leaving me shaking and making me disgusted with myself.

What the hell is wrong with you? Since when have you started screaming like a banshee?

Our staring resumed. It was a position we took often and one I hated. And then I remembered this morning's incident. "Is it because of the attempted theft in your garage?"

He waved his hand as if that incident was irrelevant, forgotten. But his eyes said differently. "There'll be many things I do you won't approve of. Pick your battles carefully, Ivy."

There it was again—that challenging tone that grated on me. And his smooth, even voice pricked me like a thousand needles.

I took a deep breath and responded calmly, "I can say the same thing to you, *Nicholas*."

"Oh, you have no idea how much I'm controlling myself already. If it were up to me, you wouldn't be leaving the house without me."

Did he just say that? "You don't own me! Treat me as your equal. Starting. Now."

"You belong to me, Ivy. Remember that." He took a step forward.

Too late. I was done. "This was a big mistake." Exhaustion hit me from our continuous fights, leaving me drained, both physically and mentally. Despite everything, we had made little headway, if any at all. "I don't belong to you. I'm not a possession."

We could never work things out, that much was certain. This wasn't the relationship I wanted. Someone controlling me and telling me what I could and couldn't do? Unacceptable.

Before he could get closer, I made a beeline for the elevator. "Sit down. We're not done," he commanded.

The sharpness of his words pushed me over the edge. "Who do you think you're talking to? I don't answer to you, so stop ordering me around. I don't have to do anything you tell me to do."

I stormed off and pressed the elevator button. The door started opening immediately, but Nick blocked me from getting in. "We've discussed this already. Stop walking out the moment things don't go your way."

I glared at him, exhaustion hitting me from every front, but damn if I back down today. "First you give me the respect I deserve. *Then* we'll talk."

He exhaled, turned me around, and pressed me against the wall. "I'm sorry for upsetting you. This whole situation is taking a completely different turn."

His first apology. My body reacted, telling me to take this as a victory. "We're very different people, Nick. I'll never agree with what you want."

He leaned in and my stupid body melted instantly. Unbeatable magnetic pull compelled me to surrender. Defying my body's needs, I balled my hands into fists so I could stop myself from touching him.

"Sending a car to your work can make or break our relationship?" he asked with complete sincerity.

"It's more that I told you to stop interfering in my personal life. Fighting like this is exhausting, Nick. Not even a week and we're arguing about something or other." I tried pushing him away, seriously doubting my decision-making skills around him.

He didn't budge. "Then stop fighting me, sweetheart. Let's sit down and talk. No fights. No walking out on me. Just explain to me and hear me out."

I resigned myself to what he wanted. For once, he was right.

Nick moved aside, letting me walk back into the apartment. I reached the terrace and slumped into the lounge chair. Now that the sun has gone down and with the open sky, it felt chilly. But the breeze helped. I was grateful that Nick didn't follow. I needed time to collect my thoughts.

Eventually, he joined me and wrapped a soft blanket around me. His thoughtfulness should have melted my heart, but it didn't. Not even with his jacket and vest gone, shirt untucked, tie missing, and top buttons undone, revealing his chest and neck that I had kissed at least a hundred times between last night and this morning.

Before lascivious thoughts could fill my head, I concentrated on our issues. "I want you to respect my boundaries."

"Okay. And I want you to respect my decisions," he countered.

Furious, I almost pounced on him like a wildcat, but he went on: "At the very least, I expect you to come talk to me."

"What is your reason for forcing your decisions on me?"

"This city is not as safe as it used to be." Nick's voice softened.

"Yet millions of people call Manhattan their home," I argued.

"What happens to other people doesn't concern me. You are my..." He stopped mid-sentence and reached for my hand. "You're the only person who matters to me."

Was that genuine concern in his voice? I stared at his face, his eyes. He wasn't faking the unease. About what, though?

"What am I missing, Nick? You can't possibly keep me safe every minute of every day."

"But I'll try, with whatever is in my control." He scooped me into his lap. I didn't resist. The concern in his eyes, the crease on his forehead, made it clear—he wasn't faking it. "Ivy, you can't run away every time something doesn't go your way —not if you expect me to respect your boundaries. Relationships need communication."

"That's something I agree with. But I hate it when you interfere without asking me first." Taking his face between my hands, I kissed his forehead. "I'll try not to walk away, but I still don't want the car."

"That's non-negotiable, Ivy. Do this for my peace of mind."

Frustrated, I sat up straight. "What're you protecting me from? Car thieves? Millions use the subway daily without issues."

"You're not just anyone. Let this one go. Do it for me, please." He again evaded my question about this morning.

"But why? Even Ryan never got weird about me using public transportation."

"Sweetheart, you aren't just Ryan's sister anymore."

"And what's that supposed to mean?"

After a weighty pause, he got down to explaining, "My status comes with a price, including enemies. Keeping you safe is my top priority."

"And this is the price I pay to be with you?"

"Maybe," he replied, almost saying yes, but stopping at the very last second.

Torn between my independence and his need to control my every step, I wasn't sure where we were headed. Ryan was protective, but Nick's paranoia was on another level. His portfolio was undoubtedly bigger than the McAlister Group, but could I see myself fitting into his lifestyle? Another change I hadn't considered.

But you want to be with Nick.

"I didn't tell you where I was. How did you find me?" I asked my next question, gnawing at him.

"Can we please not start another fight tonight?" he pleaded.

"You embarrassed me in front of my friends. I deserve to know."

"I wouldn't have come if you had answered my messages."

"Nick, you sent a car without asking, you barged into the restaurant unannounced, somehow knowing where I was, and you were rude to my friends. Do you think any of this is acceptable?" I challenged him, not ready to let go.

His shoulders slumped. "You would've known if you checked your messages. Ivy. This is so fucked up, I never had to explain myself to anyone before."

"Then you were dating doormats." I ignored the rest.

"Clearly."

Frustration bubbled inside me, but I took a deep breath to calm my nerves. "You're not used to being called out. I'm not used to being controlled. We both have to adjust. If you want me to change, you need to change too. And this is non-negotiable."

"For you, sweetheart, I'm open to anything," Nick said, looking down at our hands.

At least we had one thing in common: we both wanted this relationship to work. Even though I felt it was a mistake, deep down, I knew it wasn't. Unlike couples attuned to each other, we faced a rocky road ahead. Yet, I would be lying to myself if I said I wanted anyone else the way I wanted Nick.

"I've been set in my ways far too long," he said.

"I get it—you need a runway, not a quick launch." That made sense. It also meant we had a long road ahead of us. "You need to make an effort with my friends, too. They're important to me." I stated my next point.

"Promise not to walk out or ignore my messages and you got yourself a deal."

No kidding. I extended my hand to seal the deal and put an end to the negotiation. He grabbed me, drawing me into a tight embrace. His face came closer and closer until it got blurry and I was nothing more than a bag of sensation. His lips touched mine, first gently and then mercilessly, silencing me from uttering another word. My heart raced from zero to a hundred.

Nick's kisses grew demanding, asking me to join him, lose myself in him. My fingers tore at his shirt, making buttons fly. Lust sparked across my skin. The straps of my dress and my bra shredded. His mouth latched on to my puckered nipples, teasing with his tongue and teeth until they glistened with his saliva and stood at attention.

"You are infuriating. If only you did what you're told." His lips paused so he could taunt me.

I bit his shoulder, hard, wanting him to feel the pain tomorrow when I drove off in that car. "You are exasperating. Why can't you be a normal person?" I complained, after marking him.

"Normal or not, you still want me." He winked and sucked my bottom lip between his own. His hands left my breasts, moving up and down my bare back. He encircled me in his arms, pulling me into him as if there was any space left in-between. His every touch was an aphrodisiac to my soul. I hated him and loved him with the same passion and intensity.

"This is not what I envisioned." Undone by his relentless torture, my libido hummed back to life. Only Nick could spark this, could short-circuit my brain. I burned for this man, the ache deep under my belly confirmed.

"Too late to change your mind, sweetheart. You are all mine."

His hands traveled over my back, my waist, and my shoulders, as if he couldn't settle on where to touch first. He wasn't getting enough. His chest pressed against my breasts, and the sensation was electric. I was melting under his every touch, but his galling mouth pushed my buttons.

"Don't be so sure." I dug my nails deep into his back, scraping his skin and trying to inflict physical pain to compensate for his rankling mouth.

Our eyes met; our mouths crashed. The logical side of my brain started shutting down. All I wanted was Nick and his cock deep inside of me. He ripped away my lace panties. I kissed every inch of his face and tugged his hair to make damn sure he was in pain. He didn't complain, and that infuriated me as well.

Nick carried me inside the apartment like I weighed

nothing. I firmly wrapped my legs around his waist, with my torn dress pooling between us. My physical need was maddening. He undid his zipper, pulling his cock free, and thrust hard into me against the glass wall.

He moved with stealth and animalistic fury. I panted under his furious push for a release. This wasn't love; it was pure primal need. Nick's harsh grunts matched my every raspy groan. We were there, together, every step of the way. He pushed his shaft deeper, beyond anything I had ever felt—undulating my nerves, irresistibly intoxicating, taking me to an unexplored domain.

"I'll fuck your brains out until you stop defying me." Nick's hoarse voice had that residual irritation and a wild need to control me. If I could only shut his pretty mouth.

"I'll get you on your knees and have you begging me first," I told him, between groans.

My core convulsed with heady pleasure. His guttural growls followed. Lost in the sensation, a powerful orgasm made its way through my core. With a fervent cry, I climaxed, my entire body tensing as my release exploded through me.

Finding his own release, Nick came inside of me. He buried his face in the crook of my neck. "Ivy!" he called out raggedly.

Gasping for air, we stayed entangled in each other's arms. Our eyes met, savoring the lingering pleasure.

"You're going to ruin me," Nick murmured, and rested his sweat-laden forehead on my shoulder.

Chapter Nine

A green satin nightgown lay on the bed when I emerged from the shower. The color matched the deepest part of Nick's iris, like a wild landscape of a summer afternoon.

"No T-shirt tonight?" I inquired.

"I don't want my staff seeing you in just a shirt again."

"Wasn't that fun?" I winked and walked past him to pick up the nightgown. The fabric was sleek as water when I wore it, but defeated the purpose. What exactly could I possibly hide under this negligee of a cloth that barely managed to cover my nipples on the top and my ass on the bottom? Part of me felt more exposed than I had been in his shirt.

Nick came up from behind and wrapped me in a matching robe , shooting me a disapproving look and making me burst into laughter.

"I never pegged you as a Neanderthal," I teased.

"With you, I am. I can't stand the idea of another man seeing you again."

"Is that right?" I mocked him.

"And it will be easier if you have your clothes here. No more rushing around in the morning."

"How thoughtful." I hugged him and kissed his dimple. His smiles were a rare occasion, and I intended to enjoy it fully. "When did you have time to shop?"

"I called my stylist. He dropped off the packages at the apartment."

Of course. Since my mother's demise, no one had shopped for me. It was a mother-daughter thing that I had once cherished. His stylist buying something for me, especially something so intimate, seemed impersonal and cold, but I let it slide. "Must be nice to have people at your beck and call."

I was halfway through tying my robe when Nick scooped me up and I squealed. "With you, Ivy, no good deed goes unpunished. Check the closet and then complain. Mrs. Martinez has worked all evening on it."

"Yes, *sir*," I mocked, saluting as he put me on the bed.

He kissed the crown of my head and pulled me into his chest. Like the night before, my arms possessively wrapped around him. We had a long way to go until we fully understood each other and learned to coexist. For now, I was happy that we were together.

"Just because you and Ryan don't indulge doesn't make you any less rich."

"Not rich enough to avoid New York subways," I said, innocently fluttering my eyelashes.

"Give it a rest, sweetheart. I had a long day." He threw his arm over his forehead as he closed his eyes in exhaustion.

"Hey..." I placed my hand on his chest, gazing up at his face. "Is everything all right?"

"It's work."

"Is it about the audit meeting?"

His eyes flew open, confusion flickering before he remembered I was there during his morning calls. Pulling me closer, he sighed. "I don't want you to worry. You're here now and starting a new job. You should be happy with your decisions."

"I'm happy, Nick. I always wanted this."

"Good. You aren't going anywhere anyways."

"You can share your worries with me, too. Relationship means sharing everything, not just good times." Relationship rule one-oh-one. Did I have to say it out loud?

He smiled, kissing my forehead. "I'd like to share everything with you, sweetheart. But not on our third day and definitely not these mediocre things." When I didn't respond, he explained, "I'm trying to wrap my hands around it. I hate getting into situations I can't control. Trying to nip it in the bud before it becomes a headache."

"Want to watch the game?" I suggested, hoping to distract him. We'd had a rough evening, I couldn't blame him if he just wanted to relax. This time I met with a look of surprise. I smiled. "What? You don't watch soccer anymore?"

"Not as much as I would love to. I'm surprised you remember." His smile broadened.

"How can I forget Captain Nick Branson, center midfield, minimum one goal per game?"

He got up from the bed and returned with the TV remote. "Do you remember all the rules?"

"We'll find out soon enough. You guys discussed every strategy with me before your games," I said, thinking back to those days when Ryan and Nick were part of their university team and they took it upon themselves educating me on the sports.

"Good times. I thought you didn't like soccer." His eyes

were on the remote, flicking through channels until he found ESPN.

"I pretended not to. That was half the fun."

"You're evil." Nick pulled me with him and we settled on the couch in front of the fireplace. A large television screen mounted over the mantelpiece came to life. Mexico was leading with thirty-nine minutes left, and the USA definitely wasn't playing at their best.

Nick's excitement was palpable as he started his commentary. He ranted about one player's terrible season and another's obsession with commercials. Lost in his excitement, he missed the winning goal. USA lost, but he seemed relaxed.

When he wasn't controlling, Nick was funny and loving. This side of him was reserved for a select few, and I was lucky to be one of them. I wished more people could see how amazing he truly was.

After the game we went to bed, tangled up like the night before. No matter how my day went, ending it in Nick's arms was always perfect.

———

NICK WOKE ME TO THE SOUND OF THE ALARM AT half-past six. He carried me to the bathroom and set me down before turning on the shower. We brushed our teeth together at the sink. It was only when I looked into the foggy mirror that I noticed all the marks on his body. Turning him around, I inspected his back where my nail marks were the most prominent. The scar on his bicep paled in comparison, at least for now.

"Seems like you have a lot to hide today." I traced one long mark that ran down his back, feeling guilty now that my anger subsided.

"A memorable night. One I don't want to forget for a long time." He took my hand and softly kissed my fingers. "I always knew you were a crazy wildling."

I chucked. "It's your fault for bringing the worst out of me."

"That's unfortunate. You bring the best in me." Nick pulled me into a firm embrace until my body molded into his. Our fight from last night had taken a toll on us. Who would have imagined brand new relationships could have so much turmoil? I realized our learning curve was too rocky.

In the shower, Nick gave me a massage. It was his way of apologizing. His every caress, the feel of his hands on my skin, and the way his fingers stroked my hair were heavenly. He went down on me, and my breathing turned erratic.

Sitting in front of me, Nick's mouth started nudging the lips of my sex. He circled my clitoris with his thumb pad, slower and then faster. His tongue delved inside my soaking cleft. Shamelessly, I opened myself to the pleasure and the brewing climax. Nick parted my legs wider and repositioned me. Draping one leg over his shoulder, his tongue traveled deeper inside of me. The mind-numbing pleasure continued until I screamed out and climaxed in his mouth.

NICK QUICKLY DRIED HIMSELF BEFORE HELPING ME to do the same in leisure. I brought him up to speed about my plans for the evening.

"Remember, Ryan and Risha are coming back today. I'm spending the evening with them and staying over at his place."

"Noted. Let's get ready. I don't want you to be late on your second day of work." He kissed the crown of my head as we left the bathroom together.

He didn't say so, but it was clear he hated the idea of being away from me. The feeling was mutual, but my plan was unavoidable. Initially, I returned to Manhattan to spend a week with Ryan. Day one, he went missing because he was proposing to Risha. Day two, they had an engagement party, and right after they left for the Caribbean islands. I needed an evening with my brother, even though a part of me wanted to be with Nick.

But as soon as I walked inside Nick's closet, I forgot about Ryan and the evening plans altogether. Half of the place had now transformed into a sartorial heaven with brand new clothes, two full racks of shoes, and a collection of designer handbags. I opened drawers that were filled with jewelry and lingerie. Shocked, I looked up at him with my mouth agape.

He caught my reaction and his face lit up. "Please don't tell me you're not impressed and I need to fire my stylist. I kind of like him."

I knew Nick was trying to impress me, waiting for a pat on the back. I made him happy. "Fire him? I'm about to tell you to keep him forever!"

I checked out my new wardrobe. It undoubtedly met my high standards. Clothes for every occasion, from work outfits to evening wear to party attire. There were even athletic sets for my runs. Nick hadn't shopped for these clothes himself, but he had clearly spent time explaining my size and style, and my needs and wants. I giggled as I let myself get lost in the abundance of fabric, spoiled for choice as what to wear.

———

MRS. MARTINEZ, NICK'S HOUSEKEEPER, GREETED US with hot cups of macchiato on the kitchen island. She was enthusiastic and bubbly and all smiles when we met. I liked her already. She inquired if we wanted breakfast and we both declined politely.

While we took our first sips of coffee, we settled down for a quick chat before heading out. "Now that I know you're still into soccer, your favorite team is coming here to play us next month," Nick mentioned. "Want to go?"

"Italia?" My smile widened. I'd been a die-hard fan since I started watching soccer with Daddy. And it had nothing to do with my vacation in Italy.

"Only problem is we'll be supporting opposing teams."

"That's all right. As long as you're not a sore loser, we'll be fine."

Nick's laughter filled up the room. "Your team sucks."

"Look who's talking."

"Fine. Let's save the arguments for the field. Do you want to invite your friends?" he threw it so casually that I almost missed it.

My heart raced with excitement and newfound feelings for him. "You'll do that for me?"

Blowing on his coffee, Nick responded, "I aim to please, sweetheart. If that means getting approval from your friends, so be it."

"Darling, you don't need any approval. I want them to see you the way I do, and like you for who you really are." I waved my hand around him, saying, "definitely not the grouchy public persona you like to show off."

He chuckled and draped his arm around my shoulder. "Your approval is all I care about. If it matters to you, I'll definitely tone down my grouchiness."

"I want the universe to like you, Nick. For now, I'll settle for my friends to see you the way I do."

"Your wish is my command, Miss Ivy McAlister."

"Good," I said, happiness flooding me. "Now, let's go

before I decide to call in sick and lock ourselves in your bedroom for the rest of the day."

"Sick on day two may not look too good on your resume. I say, let's go." He pulled my hand to get me up with him.

I finished my coffee in a rush, thanked Mrs. Martinez, and joined Nick. He was already calling the elevator.

Chapter Ten

Transformation hit me when the elevator door opened at the garage level. Today I was standing in a high-security vault instead of a typical parking space. Sliding metal gates covered all sides of the garage area that belonged to Nick, including his private elevator that opened directly into his penthouse. The spot where his Lamborghini had been parked yesterday was empty.

"Don't you think it's overkill?" I asked, absorbing the scene.

"I can't take any chances. Yesterday's incident shouldn't have happened." We walked towards our cars, which were parked right beside each other.

"Are you like this about everything in life?"

Nick raised an eyebrow and gave me a sideways glance. "What do you mean?"

"You put metal bars in the garage, insist on a chauffeured car. How far will you go for security?"

"If there is a problem, I fix it before it becomes a nuisance. That's who I am."

"But—"

"No buts. Give it a rest, Ivy. We have gone over this far too many times."

I resigned, surrendering to the shield he was erecting around us.

———

John drove the SUV while I checked my phone to kill time during the drive to the university. There were over ten messages and at least fifty missed calls from Nick. As I started reading through them and listening to all his voicemails, I felt childish for ignoring them yesterday.

4:47 p.m.—Sweetheart, please pick up the phone. Your silence is killing me. Do this one thing for me, please.

5:50 p.m.—Ivy, this is not acceptable. Pick up your freaking phone.

7:15 p.m.—This was a serious meeting I had to attend. Thanks to you, now I have to run after you. Again.

Crap!

I immediately texted him back. **Sorry for not checking my phone yesterday. You shouldn't have missed your meeting because of me. I feel terrible.**

When he didn't respond after ten minutes, I sent him another message. **You should know I'm not happy with the car arrangement, but I'm still doing it. For you. Have a nice day. Miss you already.**

Then I sent a quick text to Ryan as well. **Home by four. See you in the evening.**

We still had at least ten more blocks to go and I was feeling guilty as shit, so I called Abby. She picked up on the first ring.

"That was fast." I said. "Did something happen or are you having a slow day at work?"

"Everything is fine. I'm heading to the cafeteria to get my caffeine fix," Abby answered cheerfully. "Before I forget, new renters came by yesterday. They want to take all the furniture along with the apartment. You okay with that?"

The Boston apartment building was owned by the McAlister Group, but to make things easier for Ryan we dealt with the local property manager directly. Not that Ryan ever got bothered by my requests, but I knew how busy he was with the business and all. Handling my own living arrangements was the least I could do.

"That's great. No problem whatsoever. When are you leaving for California?"

"As soon as we decide on an apartment. Which reminds me, my parents are planning a barbeque with some of our friends and my crazy family. It'd be nice if you join."

I pulled the phone away from my ear and looked at the screen. "You kidding? Of course I'll be there."

"I have to warn you, though. Mike is coming."

Oh, crap. Of course. Seeing Mike again would be awkward enough, but missing Abby's going away party wasn't exactly an option. "Thanks for the heads up. Mike or no Mike, I can't wait to see you."

"Me, too." I could practically see her wistful smile through the phone. The reality of it hadn't gone unnoticed by either of us. Somehow, I thought we would have more time together— at least a few more weeks before she left. "I miss you so much."

"Same," I said, feeling terrible that we couldn't talk or meet every day. In the last four years, this was the longest time we had spent apart from each other.

"Would Nick want to come?"

Abby's question made me think of my last day in Boston.

After everything that had gone down between the two men, going to Abby's on my own might be the best. "I'll check with him, but he's busy with work. It might just be me."

"Did you guys figure things out?"

Ha! Wouldn't that be the question of the day? "Let's just say we're getting there," I sighed. Nick and I had a mountain to climb before we figured each other out. For him, I was ready to put in any amount of work.

We talked about her and Parker, and my new job, until she had to get back to work, and it was time for me to get out of the car.

———

I FIRED UP MY LAPTOP AND DOVE STRAIGHT INTO MY project. Between research, arranging meetings, and compiling my report for Gwen, I barely breathed.

"Ivy, are you comfortable working solo today?" Gwen's words pulled me out of my thought process. I looked up to see her in a black pencil skirt and a white sleeveless top. She exuded effortless elegance and style. Day three with her, and I was still in awe.

"I think I have everything under control for now."

"Good. I'm heading to Boston to wrap up my move," she said, reminding me of my own things to do.

"Good luck with that. I'll have to do the same soon."

"Take time off whenever you need. This isn't your typical corporate job where you have to clock forty hours a week and request time off five months in advance."

I had the best freaking boss in the universe.

———

THE HOURS TICKED BY. MY RESEARCH KEPT ME engrossed until I heard a knock on the door. I looked up from my screen to find Rachael standing in the doorway, smiling.

I cringed when I looked down at my watch. "So sorry! I totally lost track of time." Quickly grabbing my purse from the bottom drawer, I joined her.

"I came to see where you work. It was easy to find you." Her cropped T-shirt, ripped jeans, high heel sneakers, and an oversized crossbody bag screamed effortless chic. As long as I had known Rachael, she'd always been a free spirit.

We reached the cafeteria closest to my office and picked out our salads. After paying, we took a table by the lobby. "So. Nicholas Branson, huh?" She tried to hold back a grin, but failed.

"I know, I know." I sighed. "Worst first impression, ever. Give him another chance. I promise he's amazing."

"With that face and body, he can get away with murder as well. Add the Branson name and fame, and he's a complete package, Ivy. A great catch."

I couldn't hold back my laugh. I wasn't a gold digger. My family wealth was enough for generations, but I got it, Nick was an entirely different level of rich.

"Is he why you moved back?"

I filled her in, omitting the arguments.

"Now you know everything," I finished. "To make things right he suggested going to the Italy versus USA match next month. What do you think?"

"Sounds fun! I haven't been to a game in ages. Spoiler alert, I'll be rooting for my country until my last breath."

I laughed immediately. My loyalty to the Italian team wasn't exactly a secret. "I think I'll be the odd one out, then." Being an outcast at soccer matches never deterred me from rooting for my team. My team wasn't great, but the US team wasn't entirely amazing, either.

She cleared her throat and asked, "so, is everything okay between you and Nicholas now?"

"Yes, why?"

"Well, I saw some pictures this morning and figured that maybe—"

"Pictures? What pictures?"

Taking in my confusion, Rachael removed her phone from her pocket, scrolled for a bit, and put it down on the table.

To my horror, I saw an NYZ gossip article with a picture of me and Nick at the top. It was taken last night during our heated argument. The picture made me look weak and vulnerable, with tear-filled eyes as Nick glared at me with scary intensity. The headline read, "Nicholas Branson and Ivy McAlister—NYC's new 'it' couple. But is there already trouble in paradise?"

My face flushed. This was the worst way for Ryan and Nick's parents to find out about us. I handed her the phone without looking back at her. "It wasn't like that. This pictures make it seem so bad."

"You don't have to explain," she said, and shrugged. "But do yourself a favor and subscribe to the column. Once you're in the news, they'll be sensationalizing everything you do. You should know what they're saying about you guys."

My mood was officially ruined. I put the fork down, completely abandoning the salad I had been thoroughly enjoying until now. "I didn't think of this when I moved back."

"Don't worry." Rachael squeezed my hand. "If you don't give them anything to write about, they'll get bored and move on to someone else."

I didn't know my life was exciting to begin with— until now.

AFTER SAYING GOODBYE TO RACHAEL, I CALLED NICK as I walked back to my office. His deep voice greeted me, and I could hear the muffled voices in the background.

"Sorry. I was in a meeting," Nick explained, as the noises faded and his voice got clearer.

"You're busy. We can talk later."

I was going to disconnect when I heard, "Ivy, I can't tell you how happy I am to hear your voice. Wish you'd call more often. I'm in my office now. Talk to me."

I exhaled. "There is a problem. I met Rachael for lunch, and she showed me a picture of us. It was from last night, outside Hotel Victoria."

He went silent, making me even more nervous.

"Where did you see it?"

"Some gossip site. NYZ."

"Let me call you back." The tone of his voice matched my panic. But he quickly added before disconnecting the call, "Don't worry, I'll take care of it."

I was useless in the matter, but that didn't take the apprehension away. To keep my mind occupied, I sat down at my desk and tried to bury myself at work.

After staring at Indy's home page for half an hour straight, I resigned myself to the fact that I had completely lost my focus for the day. Feeling utterly out of sorts, I left the office earlier than planned. I was worried about seeing Ryan, which was a brand-new feeling and not something I knew how to tackle.

As soon as John saw me on the walkway, he came out of the coffee shop across the building. He opened the back door for me before taking the driver's seat of the car.

To distract myself during the ride, I asked him about his life. He lived across the Hudson river with his two boys and their mother and had every intention of marrying her, but there was never a good time to propose. After all these years, they were happy with their arrangement. Love and happiness in a relationship made the rest semantics.

Unfortunately, getting to know John didn't help me feel any better. The drive didn't help. Freaking green lights didn't help. All I wanted right now was to delay the inevitable.

As I got out of the SUV, I dragged my feet along the curb. They felt too heavy, and every step seemed impossible to take.

You'll have to face Ryan, eventually. Besides, Nick and Ryan are best friends. You're overreacting. As usual.

Self-convincing didn't help.

My phone rang inside my purse, making me jump. I picked up on the second ring. "Nick?"

"It's done. You have nothing to worry about."

Relief washed over me faster than the tension that had spread during my lunch hour. "You don't know how happy you made me." I walked into a coffee shop in the next building, desperate for some caffeine and to get my normalcy back. "That was close."

Nick cleared his throat. "Too close. Last thing I want is for Ryan to find out about us like this. He would never forgive me."

"Nick, you scare me when you say stuff like that." As if I wasn't worried already.

"The dynamics are different between us, Ivy. I'm breaking all kinds of bro codes by dating his sister. Add our age difference and—"

"So what if he doesn't approve of our dating? What then?" I cut him off. And what was this "bro code?"

"I'm saying I've got to talk to Ryan and explain everything." His voice dropped a few decibels. "Us being together can be news, but it can't be a secret that blows up in our faces."

"I don't want to be in the news either. Ever," I exclaimed, annoyed.

"That's hard to control, babe."

"No, Nick! I haven't signed up for this!"

"Ivy. Stop."

His admonition halted me. I felt his frustration even through the phone, unfortunately I was feeling the same. Frustrated. This was precisely the life I wanted to avoid.

But you also wanted him.

"Let's discuss this media thing when we meet," Nick said.

He was used to being in the news, but I wasn't. My world was shifting rapidly, and I had no control over any of it. When I stayed silent, he tried changing the course of our discussion. "How is your day going?"

"It was fine until I saw that article. How are things on your end?" I ordered an espresso shot and took a seat. My annoyance wasn't ready to leave me completely. To say the least, I was feeling out of sorts from the rumors and pictures on the gossip site and from being worried about meeting my own brother. That definitely wasn't me.

"Let me make you feel better. How about we meet after your dinner?"

I laughed at that insane idea. He wasn't joking. "The answer is no. I gotta go now."

"Not so fast." His chair creaked and our conversation continued. "Thank you for agreeing to the car."

"I'm doing it for you," I reminded him again and bent backward in my seat. "Is your crisis under control now?"

"There are things we need to discuss; my work isn't one of them. But to give you some insight, we're accessing it. Nothing you should worry about."

His voice didn't match his words. I had a nagging feeling that it was more serious than he was letting on. And what was that thing to discuss? Was he again going back to moving in with him, since we had crossed the two-day mark now? I wasn't ready to discuss it yet, so I concentrated on the rest of our discussion. "Are you sure there's nothing I can do to help?"

"Sweetheart, my team is working around the clock. I pay them well to make sure you and I don't have to worry."

Fine, he didn't want me to worry. He had his entire team behind him, and maybe I was overthinking. "Thanks for handling the picture. And for calling. I feel much better now."

"Meant what I said, sweetheart. I love hearing your voice."

"Me, too." I was sure my cheeks changed color when his voice softened like that. "Rachael wants to go to the game with us."

"Great. I can't wait to spend time with your friends and see your team lose."

"You're cute when you're wrong. Later, baby."

I finished up my espresso, got myself an oatmeal cookie, and made my way to Ryan's apartment with renewed confidence.

Chapter Eleven

Instead of unlocking the penthouse door, I rang the bell. Ryan immediately welcomed me with a bear hug—a gesture I'd grown accustomed to since my childhood. His tall frame had been a constant, but his facial hair was a recent addition. My brother could pull off any darn look effortlessly. Thanks to our McAlister genes, he could be in rags and still set a fashion trend.

After a moment, Risha joined us.

"Welcome back! You both look so tan!" I announced as I entered.

We settled down on a pristine white couch in a very retro bohemian living area. The light from the wide-open windows, the brightness of the accent walls, and the Zen paintings brought new life into this home. I couldn't find my parents here, but I saw a very loving couple and a healthy, wholesome relationship.

"Well, being South Asian American, I'm already pretty tan. Can't get any tanner than this," Risha laughed, running her fingers over her bare forearm.

Her light olive skin contrasted against her white halter top and shorts, and complemented her long black hair tied back in a bun. She even carried *casual* with elegance. After meeting Risha, I understood why my brother didn't date just anyone. He was looking for beauty and intelligence, and grace and sophistication. My soon-to-be sister-in-law had it all.

"I'm so jealous of your skin. Instead of tanning, I burn." I removed a small box out of my purse and handed it to Risha. "You guys tossed so many surprises my way that I couldn't get you a gift until today. Welcome to the family, Risha."

Risha looked at Ryan, but made no attempt to take the box from me. "You didn't have to get me anything, Ivy."

"I wanted to. It's something close to my heart and I want to give it to someone who deserves it."

And it's not a bribe for when Ryan learns of my relationship with Nick. Or the fact that I would never join my family business.

She opened the blue velvet box, her eyes widening at the diamond stud earrings inside. Her reaction brought me back to the present. Risha's engagement ring belonged to Mom. I was glad Ryan found the person who deserved it. The earrings had come with it.

"Mom always wanted you to have the earrings," Ryan reminded me.

"I had them. Now I want Risha to have them. Please, Ryan, don't say no. Memories are more precious to me than anything tangible. Besides, I want to give Risha something that means something to me." I turned to Risha. "I'm not much of a gift-giver. You may not get another one for a long time."

"Yet every gift you give is something special," Ryan said, sitting beside Risha.

I shrugged and smiled, then I told Risha the significance of it. "Dad gave these earrings to Mom on their first anniversary. I can't think of a better engagement gift for my sister-in-law to be."

Risha looked for Ryan's approval. When he nodded, she turned to me and said, "You made this priceless, Ivy. I can't tell you how happy I am to be part of this family."

———

I GROUP HUG LATER WE SETTLED DOWN ON THE couch. Ryan prepared drinks for us. One vacation story followed another, laughter filling the house like a long-lost melody. I couldn't even remember the last time we laughed so much in these rooms. They were all tainted by sadness and the most miserable time of our lives.

"What are you ladies in the mood for? Dining out or ordering in?" Ryan asked, glancing between us.

Risha turned to me. "What do you think?"

"I had a crazy day, so I wouldn't mind chilling in the house and ordering in." That wasn't far from the truth. Mostly, I wanted to avoid photographers. Hopefully, staying out of the spotlight for a few days would give Nick time to talk to Ryan and set things right.

Our food arrived. We delved into Risha's trip stories, photos, and beautiful, albeit private, love story with Ryan. Eventually, I decided to share some of my own news as well.

Handing my empty glass to Ryan for a refill, I said in one breath: "I've moved back to New York permanently, and transferred to Columbia."

With my heart in my throat, I waited for Ryan's reaction. It took them both a few seconds to process what I'd said. Ryan's initial shock turned into another bear hug. "This is serious news, Ivy. What made you change your mind?"

"I went back to Boston after your engagement party.

Talking to Abby made me realize it was time for a new start for me. Everyone's moving on, so why not me? And why not here?"

"Don't get me wrong, I'm very happy with your decision, just a little shocked. Until a week ago you were adamant about not leaving Boston. But now you've already moved back?" Ryan pressed further. "What about Mike? Weren't you guys planning to move in together?"

"It didn't work out." I knotted my fingers as guilt weighed in on me.

His expression turned to relief, like he was waiting for me to make that decision on my own.

"Glad to have you here, Ivy." Risha squeezed my hand. "I'm also happy you're not settling for anything less than what you deserve." I looked up to meet her eyes. She tapped my hand and smiled. "You deserve the world, Ivy. Go for what your heart desires."

I nodded because she saw right through my carefully crafted façade. That was something Ryan couldn't do. Women could understand their own, and I realized my sister-in-law couldn't be easily fooled. But did she know who I had actually moved here for? Ryan was too elated to see anything beyond his excitement. I had fulfilled his wish by returning home.

Liquor flowed and laughter continued. Risha kept us entertained with stories. Our dinner comprised authentic cheeseburgers, which were eaten on the couch while we watched a new Marvel movie.

I excused myself to change into my pajamas before starting the sequel. It felt like a full-circle moment, reminiscent of happier times before our parents passed.

"You're sleeping over, right?" Ryan asked as I headed to my old bedroom.

"Of course, for tonight. Tomorrow I'll move into a hotel until I find an apartment."

"You stay here until you find something you like," Ryan said.

My Real Estate Tycoon brother wouldn't let me live in an apartment that McAlister Group didn't own, but I was playing a game of my own. I wanted to be with Nick as soon as I could. "Seriously, Ryan. I don't want to intrude."

"You're not intruding. I'm ecstatic that you're back," Ryan said. "But be honest with me. How did you come to change your mind within a week, when I couldn't convince you for years?"

I swallowed hard and reminded him of MoxTo's inauguration party the day I landed in Manhattan. "Well, I met Professor Sinclair at your hotel's opening last weekend. She's at Columbia now, and I've been wanting to take her class."

"So, it was the professor who changed your mind? Does that mean you're going to work with me now?"

How are those two things connected?

"No, Ryan."

"Why not?"

"Because Gwen also asked me to be her assistant. I started few days ago."

Ryan thought for a moment, making me wonder what was next. "I'm happy it all worked out for you. Let's reconvene after the summer and talk about your future plans." Before I could stop him, he added, "We can spend the entire night discussing it as well."

I shook my head. "After the summer is over. Let me work with Gwen for now."

I will never work with you. The words were stuck to my tongue, but he gave me some time to deliver the news, and I seized the opportunity.

I turned on my heel, heading to my bedroom, when Ryan's voice stopped me mid-stride. "Just so you know, Gwen is on Nick's payroll."

Stunned, I faced him. "What do you mean?"

"She's been working for Nick for years now. Besides her university job, of course."

It felt like someone had pulled the rug from under me. I tried to make sense of it because I never saw this coming. "Gwen told me she does consultations for many clients."

"She does. We consult her as well, but she is on a retainer with Nick. He invests in startups and Gwen's expertise comes in to increase their profitability. They're a team."

The realization hit me like a punch. Nick had introduced us. He told me many times to join Columbia because Gwen was here. Xavier had offered to pull some strings to help me get into Columbia. All of it hit me at once. I couldn't breathe. I couldn't feel my feet. Was I sitting down on the floor or still standing?

Could Nick have orchestrated all of this from the beginning? Was he responsible for Gwen changing jobs as well? He knew I would never move to New York—so instead, he made Gwen move. That automatically influenced my decision.

I didn't want to believe it. But deep down I already knew the truth... Nick had gone to crazy lengths to control my life while I, a complete fool, hadn't even noticed.

Chapter Twelve

I didn't recall moving from the hallway into the shower, but I reached it somehow. My body operated on autopilot. My feet carried me to the bathroom, where my hands undressed me and turned the shower knob. The hot spray pelted my skin, but my lungs refused to draw breath, and my brain struggled to process the truth.

No one had ever deceived me before. In a way, life itself had deceived me by taking away my parents, but that hadn't been their fault. Nick, on the other hand, had intentionally orchestrated this whole thing. He had influenced my decision to move back to New York. He had told me he didn't get into situations where he couldn't control the outcome. And then he betrayed me by controlling my life to this extent.

His lies suffocated me.

Maybe there's something you don't know. Maybe you're jumping to conclusions.

My heart didn't believe Nick could be a bad guy. But it was impossible to ignore facts that were right in front of me. He knew how much I hated to be controlled, so he'd played it like a game of chess and I had fallen right into the trap. Did he seriously think I would never find out? How far would he have gone if Ryan had not told me tonight?

Even though my head throbbed and my heart couldn't beat, I couldn't afford to make Ryan suspicious. So, I showered, dressed, and forced a cheerful face before joining Ryan and Risha for the movie. Switching off my brain and going with the flow was easy; I had mastered that art. Ryan didn't need to know the truth. No one had to know the man I trusted the most played me.

A little after midnight, we called it a night. "Tomorrow we are heading to Princeton to meet my family," Risha announced. "They would love to have you over as well."

"Is it okay if I meet them another time? I have to handle some university stuff." Apparently, I had mastered the art of lying, too.

"Of course. Do what you have to do. Maybe you can join us for dinner when they visit the city."

"I look forward to it."

———

MEMORIES OF NICK FLOODED BACK WITH A vengeance as soon as I entered my bedroom. The space still held echoes of Mom and Dad—laughter, teasing, and joyful galore. Planning out those last few vacations that never happened. Everything came crashing down in this same room —the cops' arrival, Doug pulling me into a hug, and Ryan putting me to sleep every night with a prescription drug.

Same home, my old room, and the same pain I hadn't felt in a very long time. Either I had traveled back in time or it was some cruel *déjà vu* vortex that had sucked me in and didn't want to let me go. The reasons for my pain were completely different this time around, but it didn't hurt any less. Knowing that Nick had lied and deceived me intentionally made it hurt even more.

I couldn't believe my naivety. Nick had introduced me to Gwen. She asked me if I was Ivy McAlister when she already knew who I was. Ignorant that I was to fall for the lies and flattery Gwen fed me. Nick had hired her to do it, but she wasn't the real culprit. Nick had played me from the very beginning.

Blinded by him, by the physical chemistry, and by your adolescent dreams—you played right into his hands, Ivy.

The hurt and betrayal gnawed at me. I was at a loss for how to overcome these feelings. He had crushed me with his lies, dragging me back to the rut it had taken me almost a decade to crawl out of. The weight of his deceit felt like a vise around my chest and squeezed the air out of my lungs. All those years of therapy under my belt, yet here I was having trouble processing truth and putting things into perspective.

Sleep eluded me. My heart pounded painfully in my chest. In the dark room, sudden bursts of light and a pinging sound startled me. I stretched my hand across the bed and fumbled until I grasped my phone. Nick's message popped up, momentarily blinding me with its sudden brightness.

I'm addicted to you, sweetheart. Can't sleep without you. Please come over. I'm on my knees, begging you.

His message hit me hard. His lies, deceit, and sweet talk— they all hurt the same. After tossing, turning, and crying my heart out, I let my mind win. I switched my phone off and threw it across the room; changed into my workout clothes; scribbled a note for Ryan, saying I was going for a run, and left it on the refrigerator door.

Every sound in the building was intensified at this time of night, making me jump when the elevator door opened. I stepped into the lobby. The night security guard tipped his hat as soon as he saw me.

Instead of heading straight to Central Park, I veered right and began running south. The streets were mostly empty, with few pedestrians and sparse traffic. The sky's darkness mirrored the shadowing doubt in my heart. Streetlights illuminated the walkways, guiding my path. Without a clear direction, I ran until I reached Columbus Circle, then kept going. Navigating Manhattan became effortless. My only aim was to lose myself in the city's labyrinth.

I zigzagged through the streets, indifferent to where I was or where I might end up. As the numbered streets faded into named ones, I felt completely untethered. The anonymity of the city-street provided a welcome escape.

By the time the first rays of light pierced the sky, I found myself somewhere down south. Nick's betrayal and lies weighed more heavily on me than the fatigue from running. I had stopped crying a while back, but the pain remained like an unrelenting ache.

Desperately, I recalled my sessions with Dr. Patrick Campbell, the psychologist who had helped me navigate the darkness after my parents' death. He had taught me how to channel my negative emotions, anger, and grief into something I could handle. I believed I had shattered those emotional barriers, that I had become strong. But now that strength felt like a distant illusion; I was back to the same old Ivy.

Broken. Shattered. Defeated.

As the sun climbed higher, the streets filled with people, and they all moved with purpose. Determined strides contrasted sharply with my aimless wandering; others around me reached their destinations while I kept walking.

At a newsstand I bought a bottle of water and drank until the last drop, but it offered no relief. Nothing helped. Nick's betrayal consumed me. I tossed the empty bottle into a nearby trash can. A magazine cover caught my eye.

It was a picture of Nick and me kissing passionately. The photo, taken a week ago during Ryan's engagement party, captured us in a moment of undeniable chemistry. Our eyes closed, his arms wrapped possessively around my waist, and my hands tucked under his jacket—the image exuded intimacy and a perfect representation of how we were with each other.

The existence of this picture, though, made absolutely no sense. We were in the privacy of Nick's parents' house. Whoever took the photo had to be close—close enough to capture such an intimate moment. The magazine released it today, meaning whoever had the picture had waited a week before putting it out. The headline read, "Ivy McAlister: Nicholas Branson's New Love, or Just Another Temporary Fling?"

I picked up a copy to get a better look, but the storekeeper asked me to pay if I wanted to read it. I handed him two one-hundred-dollar bills, gathered all the copies, and threw them into the trash.

My heart was in agony, and my thoughts were tangled, unsure of what to think of everything happening around me. Seeing that picture reminded me of what we had and how we felt, adding salt to the open wound.

Nick and I had arrived in Manhattan on Wednesday, but the pictures hadn't started surfacing until Friday—the day Ryan had returned from his vacation. We had kissed each other in public on numerous occasions since then. I couldn't help but wonder what other pictures were waiting to surface and, most importantly, when and why.

My anxiety escalated into panic. Sitting down on the sidewalk, I struggled to rein in my thoughts. Too many emotions surged through me, each more overwhelming than the last. Some things I could control, but others were beyond my grasp. Being in the media spotlight was something I never anticipated, and it was something I couldn't control.

Controlling my feelings for Nick, however, was a battle of my mind. I had done it before. I could do it again. The last time I ran away with my broken heart, it took me over a year to move on... but I still couldn't forget him. This time he gave me a reason not only to forget him, but to hate him. I wanted to hate him.

A control freak to the core. I should have known we were too good to be true.

Blocking all my internal turmoil, I resumed my walk. Mindlessly crossing block after block until the Statue of Liberty came into view, I found myself in Battery Park on the southern tip of Manhattan.

The sun beat down relentlessly. It scorched my shoulders and back. The heat was unbearable, making me sweat despite the light breeze. My feet ached with each step, but I wasn't ready to head home yet.

I remembered the day when Ryan and I came here with our parents. It felt like yesterday, and even the smallest and tiniest of memories remained vivid in my mind. My parents gave in to my insistence on riding the ferryboat, and Dad bought us both cotton candy before we went over to the island to see the landmark. It had been a balmy summer morning, just like this one. We had been so happy that day.

I bought a ticket. Nostalgia engulfed me. A bittersweet moment. *I'll never get to do this with Mom and Dad ever again,* I thought sadly. However, I'd made such beautiful memories while they were alive, and I tucked them into my heart as I continued towards the ferry line.

I walked to a nearby food cart and bought a pink cotton candy before joining the line. After boarding, I made my way to the roof and took the seat where Mom and I had sat during our trip. Dad and Ryan had stayed in the back to take pictures.

The sun beat down on my shoulders today. Without sunscreen, I knew that, soon, I'd turn a shade of lobster red. I could already feel the pain that awaited me in a matter of hours, but it didn't deter me from reliving my old memories. Taking a small bite of cotton candy, I turned six years old again.

"Thank you for convincing us to come, Ivy. I have to confess; I've never been to the Statue of Liberty before."

"Then you're not a real New Yorker yet!"

"I guess I'm not, sweet pea. But I'm glad I came here to study and met the love of my life and made this beautiful family here."

"I'm glad, too, Mom. You and Dad are the best parents in the world."

She laughed with unbridled happiness that warmed my heart.

At Liberty Island, I discarded my somewhat-eaten cotton candy and took a leisurely walk. For the rest of the day, I reminisced about my past, attempting to recreate the same experience I had during my last trip here. Mom and Dad walked with me, Ryan had been so happy. We took so many pictures that day, and they were still part of the treasure trove I carried everywhere with me.

When I got back to Battery Park, my feet had already surrendered, but my mind still refused to rest. Pushing my body to its extreme limit, I continued wandering the city until darkness fell once more. Eventually, exhaustion overtook me.

I hailed a cab and headed back home.

———

THE YELLOW CAB CAME TO A SCREECHING STOP right outside Ryan's building. Nick pulled open the cab door and leaned in.

"What's going on with you?" His voice sliced through the air, igniting a storm of unwanted, unexpected emotions. When I lifted my gaze to meet his, I met with his controlled fury. I handed the cash to the driver and stepped out.

"What the hell, Ivy?" Nick brushed his fingers through his hair, frustration seeping through his every movement. "I don't even know if I should be upset or worried. What are you doing? Where've you been?"

My blood surged, pounding against my eardrums. "I want you to stop following me," I managed. Despite the turmoil raging inside me, my voice remained surprisingly calm.

"If you pick up your damn phone once in a while maybe I would." Nick exhaled. "I thought we already had this conversation."

"I don't know if I should scream at you or start crying. What I do know is I have nothing left to say to you." My words hung heavy between us. My heart grieved, but I felt nothing but disappointment and frustration.

"Here we go again." Nick rubbed the back of his neck, clearly exasperated. "She finds another reason to fight."

"Did you seriously think I would never find out? Actually, don't answer that. No more fights. I'm done." I turned to go inside my building. He held my arm.

"What does that even mean? What did I do now?" His jaw tightened, and he did everything not to lose his temper.

Passersby started giving us weird stares, but Nick didn't care. I had no interest in being around him, but it was clear he wouldn't leave, so I knew we were better off inside a cafe with a handful of people and *hopefully* lesser chances of getting caught on cameras.

"Coffee shop?" I suggested, going against my own instincts to walk away from him.

"After you," he replied flatly.

I remained as calm as my mind would allow. Walking into the café and away from prying eyes, I took a seat at the very last table.

As soon as he took the seat in front of me, I looked directly into his eyes. "Are you in any way responsible for Gwen taking a job at Columbia?"

It was only a microsecond, but I caught it. The veil fell from his perfect face, and I saw the guilt flicker in his eyes. That was all the evidence I needed to confirm my suspicions. It was foolish of my heart to hope he would say all the right things and tell me this had been nothing but a big misunderstanding. That he had nothing to do with Gwen's move. That he could never deceive me.

Clearly, my heart was wrong.

"I don't want you to contact me ever again. You are Ryan's friend, so we need to be cordial with each other. But that's where it begins and ends."

"Can we talk about this?"

Did I hear panic in his voice?

But that must've been my imagination as well. Maybe I was selectively hearing what I wanted to hear instead of what was said.

"You lost that chance already." I got up from my seat and he followed. "Another picture of ours is out. This time it's a print. I thought you should know."

He clenched his jaw. Whether it was reserved for me or for whoever had invaded our privacy in such a disgusting way, I didn't know. I didn't wait to find that out.

"Goodbye, Nick."

I left without looking back to see if he was following me. I was familiar with the drill—getting far away from him and healing my broken heart.

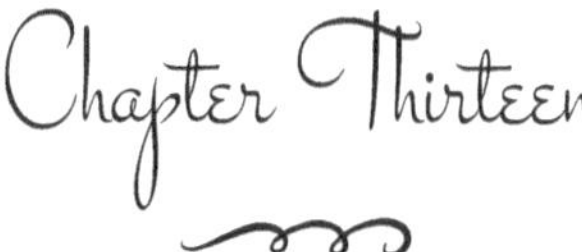

The penthouse swam in darkness when I returned almost twenty-four hours later, reminding me that Ryan and Risha were in Princeton. I went to the kitchen and memories of Nick possessed me, making it impossible to breathe.

How could I be so blinded by this attraction that I couldn't see the man he truly was? How could I let someone play me for this long?

Ryan had taken the note I left him and scribbled his own message on the back. They were going to be back before midnight, which meant I had about an hour to compose myself.

I took a long shower to wash away the sweat. Too bad the water couldn't cleanse the memories of Nick, because the ache in my chest was unbearable and left a blazing hole deep inside it. I couldn't breathe without him.

Even after what he had done to me, my heart begged me to give him a chance to explain himself. It tried to convince me that there had been some misunderstanding, that there was no way he would hurt me intentionally.

My heart was wrong.

———

"Fine," he said. "I own it."

Nick's Lamborghini was zooming down street after street, crossing every intersection with ease.

"What can I say, Ivy? Either you're not very good at research, or I'm just that good at hiding things I don't want others to know. Unless you're a market analyst and ready to spend all your time researching or reviewing financials, these things can be hard to find."

I jolted awake in the middle of the night. Nick had not lied to me about owning Blue Chip on our drive to his parents' house that day. He was simply giving me half of the truth.

His treachery had no bounds.

I wanted to scream, but no sound came out. My only wish right now was to go back to the life where Nick was nothing more than an enigma to me... to burn away all the memories of him and of our time together, so I would stop hurting.

My brain craved another run that my body wasn't capable of delivering. My stomach grumbled every few minutes, a reminder of my only meal in the last twenty-four hours had been a piece of cotton candy.

After crying my heart out again, I got up and started toward the kitchen to appease my whining stomach. Outside my bedroom, the remodel had done away with most traces of our old life. Unfortunately, now Nick filled this apartment with his memories. My body craved his touch, the searing look in his eyes every time it went down my body, and my mind couldn't think beyond him and the way he wanted to possess me. How I was going to move past this, I hadn't yet figured out.

I was munching on a mouthful of soggy cereal when Risha walked in and switched on a few lights, bringing the house back to life.

Even my favorite fruit-flavored cereal tasted bitter. I swallowed to calm my stomach.

"Did I wake you up?" I asked.

"No, you're fine. I wake up early." She entered the kitchen area and turned on the coffeemaker. "Want some?"

I nodded. "Isn't it too early for you to be awake?"

"My dad was strict about starting the day early. I guess some of his habits rubbed off on me." She removed two mugs out of a cabinet and set them down in front of me. "I also start my day early. By the time Ryan wakes up, some of my work is already done," she added with a smile.

"That's a great habit to have. My routine has been non-existent since school ended," I mentioned, trying to keep the conversation going.

Risha filled our cups with black coffee and took the seat beside me.

Setting aside my bowl of cereal, I took my first sip. "Thank you. It's good. Just the way Abby used to make it."

"You miss her?"

"More than you know." My mind traveled back to those days in Boston, sitting in the kitchen, sipping our first coffees of the day, and chatting for hours. Those days were gone forever and I couldn't shake the miserable feeling that I would never get them back. In Boston, my life was simple. Uncomplicated. No deception.

No one in Boston could hurt you because your heart was always here, Ivy.

"There are times when we feel lonely and think we can't

talk to anyone." Risha's voice brought me back to the present. "Just remember that you are not alone."

"Yeah, I know." Our eyes met, and she saw right through me. I couldn't lie to her anymore, so I told her about Nick as much as I could without bursting into tears. I had to get it off my chest, to survive another day. I was miserable.

Risha's eyes widened with shock. "What was Nick thinking?"

I couldn't be sure if she was upset with him for deceiving me or breaking the imaginary *bro code*.

"You think he played you?" she asked, keeping her hand over my arm.

Swallowing down the lump sitting in my throat, I answered, "I don't *think*, Risha. I *know*."

"You need to speak with Ryan about this."

"It's over." I resigned; headache bloomed behind my eyes. "No point telling him anything now. I shouldn't have gotten involved with Nick in the first place." I had to get past the pain somehow, to get over Nick. Nothing Ryan could do would help me get there.

"He has to know, Ivy," Risha pressed further, making me regret letting her in. "He is your brother."

Headache spread in the back of my skull. "Can I trust you to keep it between us?" I asked, half hoping she would agree. What was I thinking? Her loyalty lay with Ryan, not with me.

To my surprise, she nodded and squeezed my hand at the same time, confirming she was on my side.

Relief surged through me. I exhaled, not realizing I was holding my breath. "Thanks," I managed to say and changed the subject. "How was your dinner?"

Even though worries marred her face, she gave into my request and didn't push. She told me about their visit and all the food her mother had prepared. Her descriptions were so vivid I could almost taste the spices and smell the rich aromas of home-cooked meals. We chatted for a while and she tried all the different ways to keep my mind occupied. My broken heart only wanted Nick. My broken soul wanted to run away. The intersection of these emotions left me struggling to breathe.

At some point, Ryan left home and went to his office, even though it was a weekend. I couldn't remember the last time he had taken a week off from work. I had to agree Risha was the best thing that had happened to him in a very long time.

"I'm meeting Cece for brunch. Want to join us?" Risha asked, after putting the empty coffee mugs in the dishwasher. Cece was Taber's sister, Risha's best friend, and my close friend before I'd moved away from New York. Cece and I reconnected again at Ryan's engagement and this time, I promised her to stay in touch.

"I would love that. But I don't want to intrude."

"Don't be silly. We know each other's lives inside out. Adding a new person into the mix will do us all some good. Besides, she has a boyfriend now, Reynold." She walked over to me and gently squeezed my shoulder with both her hands. "Maybe some girl time will do you good."

She could be right. A distraction was exactly what I needed right now. "Okay. Where are we going and what should I wear?"

———

PLEASANTLY ENOUGH, OUR BRUNCH LIFTED MY MOOD. The discussion bounced between Cece's new boyfriend and her upcoming move to San Francisco. I savored the delicious food and ate until my belly was comfortably full. We chatted until we had nothing more to say.

Cece seemed aware of my relationship with Nick, but she

didn't bring it up. Whether she knew from Risha or some gossip column, I couldn't tell, but I was grateful for friends who knew when to leave things be.

My improved mood lasted until I reached home. The moment Risha and I stepped into the penthouse, I immediately knew something was off. Ryan was pacing back and forth with a Bluetooth in his ear, shouting various commands to some poor soul on the other side of the call.

His usually calm and measured voice was now strained and clipped and bouncing off the walls of the living room. The tension in the air was palpable, immediately setting me on edge. I felt like I had entered a battlefield.

Risha and I exchanged a look. The lightness from brunch evaporated quickly and was replaced with heaviness and worry. I took a deep breath and braced myself for whatever had turned our home into a pressure cooker.

"Ivy! Not so fast," he called after me, when he saw me heading to my room.

I halted and turned. My fear came to life. In the center of the table was the magazine with the picture of me and Nick on the cover.

"I trust you to tell me the truth, so I'm only going to ask you once. What is going on between you two?" he demanded, looking absolutely livid.

My hands trembled. I rubbed my sweaty palms up and down the fabric of the skirt. "Ryan, it was a big mistake. But it's over now."

"Do you know the mess you have gotten yourself into?" Ryan pointed at the picture, his eyes burning with anger.

I leaned against the wall for support. My voice quivered from the tension in the room. "Yes. But it's over. This will all go away soon," I said quietly, echoing what Rachael had told me to do—keep a low profile so that the media would back off.

I wasn't sure whether I was trying to pacify Ryan or convince myself, but my words had absolutely no effect on him. Today, my cool, composed brother was nowhere to be found.

"I trusted Nick. I trusted *you*, Ivy. And what do you do? You betray me!"

He shattered me with that statement. All the hurt and pain I had been holding inside came out in waves. My legs gave out and I slumped down onto the floor, hiding my face in my hands and sobbing uncontrollably.

"Forgive me, Ryan. I don't know what I was thinking."

"You're not a child, Ivy. Mistakes have consequences." Ryan was so mad he couldn't even stand to be in the same room with me. He stormed off to his study and slammed the door.

Risha tried to calm me down, but all I needed right now was my brother's forgiveness. Ryan's closed door told me he wasn't ready.

"Give him some time, Ivy. He's in shock," Risha told me. "Let me talk to him."

I couldn't respond. Leaving me in the living room, she walked over to Ryan's study.

Emptiness engulfed me. The dark clouds hung low until they started closing in on me, threatening to suffocate me. I cried as an image from the past began surfacing. It took every ounce of my strength to shake off that dark fear—the fear of losing whatever was left.

Once that overwhelming sense of dread subsided, I went to the kitchen and drank a glass of water. The cool liquid soothed my parched throat and helped calm my nerves, allowing me to assess the situation I had gotten myself into.

I had hurt the person who had always loved me, and fallen for a man who had done nothing but trick me and lie to me. I was having a hard time understanding myself and my life choices.

Even after an hour, the door to Ryan's study stayed shut. Giving up on any hope of resolving the issues with him today, I packed my bags and looked around for my phone. It was intact, but dead.

Not wanting to linger any longer, I dropped the charger and the phone into my bag. Bits of Ryan and Risha's heated argument emanated from the study, but I didn't interfere. I knew the cause of their argument and it was something I couldn't make peace with.

As I left home, I hastily scribbled two words on a piece of paper.

I'm sorry.

Chapter Fourteen

nother attempt at finding my place in this city, and I was on the move once again. This time, though, I wasn't running away. I hailed a cab and checked into the first hotel I stumbled upon in Times Square. I could've gone to any of the McAlister Hotels, especially MoxTo, since it was only a block away; but right now, I needed some distance from everyone.

Once settled in my room, I plugged in my phone to charge, and hopped in the shower. I had a mental to-do list and taking care of my mental health was at the very top of it.

By the time I came out of the shower, my phone was fully charged. Nick's messages from the last few days started appearing on my screen. I deleted them without checking. There was no way I was going to give that man another second of my time.

And there was not a single message from Ryan. He was upset; I got that, but I had no intention of alienating him. Whatever I had to do for his forgiveness, I fully intended to do it.

I texted him my whereabouts. **Still need to find an apartment. Would love your input, but I won't blame you if you don't want to help me right now.**

I sent him the hotel address and my room number, so he'd know I wasn't far in case he wanted to meet and work things out. Next on my list was Gwen – but then a sharp knock on the door startled me. Distracted, I opened the door without checking through the peephole.

Big mistake. Huge.

"You've got to be kidding me." Exasperated, I tried to shut the door, but Nick held it tight.

"Let's talk."

I could've screamed, cried, made a scene, and gotten him to leave, but it wasn't getting me anywhere. I was hurting badly because my heart wanted Nick. It was my ego that was numbing the pain so I could survive. I moved aside, giving him the way.

He took a seat on one side of the couch, leaving the remaining space for me. The room suddenly felt too small, even for a suite. I walked to the window, needing space to breathe. It wasn't enough.

"How did you find me?" I asked my first of many questions. My voice was tight with anxiety.

"Does that really matter?" His nonchalant tone grated on my nerves.

"You can answer or you can leave. The choice is yours."

After a moment's hesitation, he relented. "Fine. I tracked your phone."

Seriously? His admission tore me apart inside, yet he showed no remorse. As if I needed more proof that he controlled my every move.

"So much for privacy. How long has this been going on?" I demanded.

"Is this your burning question of the hour?" he deflected.

I folded my arms in front of me and waited.

He ran his fingers through his hair and huffed. "Back in Boston when I asked for your phone."

"Unbelievable." Incredulously, I threw my hands up in the air. "I trusted you with my phone you control freak! How could you do something like this?"

"Last time, five of my men spent forty-eight hours searching for you. I can't go through that again, Ivy. Keeping you safe is important to me, and I can't do that unless I know where you are. If that makes me controlling, so be it."

"You are being paranoid. Actually, you might be borderline crazy," I shot back.

"Maybe you're right. If it makes you feel better, you can track my phone, too," he offered.

"Please. I'm not a lunatic," I spat out. "Did you buy Blue Chip Corporation when I started interning for them?"

"Sure you want to go there?" His response sounded like a warning, but I was determined to uncover the truth, no matter how frightening it might be.

"I do."

He relaxed his back on the couch before starting to talk. "Okay. Not only Blue Chip, I bought every company you have ever interned at. I have a division that invests in these startups. It's the most profitable division we have created in the last couple of years."

"So, it was all for profitability? You saw how lucrative these businesses could be and you jumped on it?" I tried to grasp his motives, hoping it was all purely business driven.

We had known each other for decades, sharing countless conversations on business, world affairs, and economics. Anyone could have been born into money, but we both strongly believed it was what you did with that money that defined you. Nick was a visionary. And I hoped all the things I had been accusing him of had nothing to do with me and everything to do with business.

"If I tell you the truth, you will call me controlling again."

"I only want the truth, Nick. Give me straight."

"All right. You showed me the way, but nothing I did was for profit. I care about those businesses doing well, sure, but the profit came on its own and it was all because of you." He let his words hang in the air. "I want you to join me and head the department someday."

"That's presumptuous of you, don't you think? I don't even work for my company, how did you assume I would ever work for yours?"

"I assumed nothing, Ivy. I simply created a business you dreamed of," Nick replied calmly. Was he always paying so much attention to everything I said?

"How did you find out I wanted to be in Gwen's class? And how did you get her hired at Columbia?" I pressed further. My list was too long.

He exhaled, stood up, and went to the fridge to grab a bottle of water. He took his time, leaning against the wall before speaking again. "You told Ryan many times how much you loved Gwen's seminars. I hired her when I found out. I know the university board. One phone call was all it took."

"And then you made Gwen do your dirty work? Make me transfer and work for you?"

"I never asked Gwen to hire you. I only wanted you back."

"At what cost?" I asked, choking on that lump of pain again. I was hurting from his deceit, from the truth, and from his every admission. Nothing he said made me feel any better about the situation I had gotten myself into.

Giving up on any hope of being with Nick again, I walked to the door and unlocked it for him. "You can leave now."

"Would you have come back if I asked you to?"

A question from a lifetime ago that kept me awake at night. But he had not asked then, and it was too late for him to ask me now. "I guess we'll never find out."

"You wanted the truth, Ivy, and I gave it to you. Why can't I get the same in return?" His eyes softened. Beneath all the chaos, control, maddening antics, there remained a man with undeniably deep feelings for me.

My heart crushed inside my chest when I responded back. "Thank you for being honest for once. You can leave now."

"You wanted to be with me." His voice filled with hurt, matching my internal turmoil. Though reasons were completely opposite, feelings were the same.

"You've hurt my pride, Nick. Whatever we had, it ends right here. I'll never forgive you for what you've done."

Nick looked into my face, trying to find the hidden lies. When I didn't let him see, he came closer and wrapped me in his arms. "You didn't belong in Boston, Ivy. I agree, I should've asked you to come back. I should've been more honest. But I was scared."

"Scared? Of what?"

"That you'll say no. That you need more time. Let this go, sweetheart," he pleaded.

Sweetheart. Once an endearing word, it now felt like a thorn in my heart. He tightened the embrace, enveloping me in his warmth. Unfortunately, I couldn't give in to it. As far as I was concerned, we were strangers. And that freaking hurt.

"Let this go? Why? So, you can keep controlling me?"

"I can't control you, Ivy. And I don't want to. The only thing I want is for us to be together. I want you safe and I want you with me. Sure, you changed universities, but you've also got your professor. Your best friend is leaving Boston, too. Why are you letting your ego stop us from being happy?"

I took a step back, but I only moved as much as Nick's arms would allow. I shut my eyes to get past the pain, but to no avail. "You took away my right to choose, Nick. You decided *for* me."

When no response came from him, I had to decide. And I did. "If you ever had true feelings for me, you'll leave this room right now."

Nick's grip loosened enough to confirm he had heard me, but he still didn't let go.

"And you will never contact me again," I said with finality.

"Don't shut me out, Ivy. We can work this out and—"

The door to the room banged open, almost hitting us. "You have some nerve, asshole!"

Nick and I turned at the same time, and he started to pull me behind him. "Ryan!" I cried. "I'm sorry."

"Look Ryan," Nick began. "I wanted to tell you in person, but—"

But Ryan shouted him down. "What could you possibly say to change my mind about you? You can have your fun with any girl you want, and you decide to *seduce my sister?*"

Ryan was nothing short of enraged. I was having a hard time breathing again. This was a colossal mess that I had brought upon myself, and upon Ryan, and upon Nick as well.

"I would never hurt Ivy. You have to believe me," Nick said, trying to reason with him.

"Believe you?" Ryan snickered. He turned his head towards me. "Do you have any idea what kind of man he is?"

"Stop, Ryan. Both of you, please stop!"

"You." Ignoring me, Ryan rammed his finger into the center of Nick's chest. "Leave right now. Don't you so much as *look* at Ivy ever again."

Shocked by Ryan's outburst, Nick faced me. "Is that what you want, Ivy?"

Ryan waited, seething and enraged. For once, the decision was mine to make.

At that moment, I hated Nick with all my might... but I had loved him with the same passion all my life. I still loved him, even though he had hurt me. The heart that had always belonged to him, the heart he had broken and never thought twice about. He had hurt me in ways no one else ever did or ever could.

His dominion, his lies—there were no limits to how far he would go to get what he wanted. That was the man I had fallen in love with.

What I needed was time to heal my heart.

"Whatever we had, it's over," I heard myself saying.

"Think before you answer, Ivy." Nick took one last step toward me. "If I leave now, I'll never come back."

I felt his white-hot gaze on me, questioning my decision and warning me to think before uttering my next word. When I found the strength to accost him, I realized his mask was back on and he was devoid of love. If he ever had any feelings for me, I couldn't see them anymore.

Masking my hurt with disgust, I opened the door and waited for him to leave.

Which he did.

The door fell shut behind him.

Chapter Fifteen

"You too, Ryan. Please go. I need to be alone right now."

Ryan left without saying a word. After the door closed again, I cried my heart out, not knowing how to get past this pain and anguish or how to get over my heartbreak.

If only I could return to the life where Nick had been nothing but a dream and live in that fantasy where my life was perfect and happy with him by my side. Where I found peace in his arms. Where there were no lies and no deceit. I had loved that dream, and the time we spent together there, until the truth came out and I saw the charade.

Reality was painful and full of heartache.

———

"Ryan!" Our house was dark. Too dark to even see my fingers in my lap. But I saw him enter through the door, and that's when I got up and ran after him.

"There has been a mistake," I told him, breathlessly. "We

have to go to the hospital and verify. I've been trying to call them both, but they're not picking up their phones. That means nothing, right?"

Ryan stayed silent.

"They could be somewhere—maybe they can't hear their phones ringing. Maybe they forgot to charge their phones. There has to be an explanation!" The anxious words flowed out of me.

Ryan flipped on the light switch. The sudden glare hit my eyes and I squinted, momentarily losing my train of thought.

"Ivy..." Ryan took a step toward me. He was crying. But that couldn't be. Ryan never cried.

"It's all a big misunderstanding," I insisted. "I'm sure Mom and Dad are on their way. There's a perfectly good explanation for why they're not picking up their phones. Let's go. They weren't letting me go alone, so I was waiting for you."

"Ivy, they're gone."

I jumped to my feet when the doorbell rang. "See? They're home already!" I ran to the door, ready to greet them, ready to give them the biggest hug and make them promise to always pick up their phones when I called.

"Mom—"

"Oh, Ivy, dear. I am so sorry." A teary-eyed Rosanne, Mom's best friend and Nick's mother, pulled me into her arms.

What was wrong with everyone?

"Where are my parents, Rosanne? They're not answering my calls."

"They're dead, Ivy." Ryan's voice reverberated through my heart. "Our parents are dead."

"Sweetheart!"

My eyes flew open as I broke through the gut-wrenching nightmare. I sat up, panting, and gasped for breath. My heart contracted, and I barely drew a full breath. The darkness closed in, suffocating me. I desperately scanned my surroundings for the elusive light switch. All the while making every effort to stop the shivers and the heart palpitations. I still couldn't breathe.

"No, no, no," I mumbled. The lingering effect clung to me, leaving me shaken even after I was awake. I couldn't believe it had come back. Disoriented, I reached out until my fingers touched the cold screen of my phone—and right at that moment it started ringing, shattering the calm that was precariously standing between reality and my tormented dream. With shaking hands, I picked up the phone and pressed it to my ear.

"Nick?" My voice trembled and rolled out in a whisper.

"No, it's Abby! I've been trying to reach you for the last hour. Where were you?"

"Ab - Abby?" My voice felt so distant, like it belonged to someone else. Even though the words were mine, I couldn't recognize them.

I pushed the blanket aside and sat up straight. With my phone tucked between my ear and my shoulder, I found the bedside lamp switch. The room filled with a warm, soft glow, grounding me to the present. It took a few more seconds to realize where I was.

"Are you listening to me or am I talking to myself here?" Abby once again announced her presence on the phone.

"Sorry. I was in a deep sleep. I just woke up. What time is it?" I got off the bed, going around the room and switching on all the lights.

"Everything okay? Don't tell me you..."

"Yeah." I wiped the sweat droplets that had collected on my forehead with the back of my hand. "It was that same nightmare... it's back."

I put my phone on speaker and went to the fridge. Removing a large bottle of water, I took a few big swigs.

Cold water didn't entirely take away the anxiety, but it helped.

"I'm so sorry," I heard Abby say, her concern discernable. "What triggered it? Are you alone?"

Everything that had created this nightmare came into focus at once. My body slumped, taking away the remnants of my existence. Raw and gutted, I felt so numb.

"Ivy? Are you there?"

"Sorry, no... I mean, yes. I'm alone. Nick's voice in my dream woke me up. I'm okay now."

"You're freaking me out, girl. Why are you alone? Where is Nick? Where's Ryan? Where the hell are your friends?"

Her questions floated around over me, but my brain couldn't process a thing. It felt like someone had opened up the floodgates and I had no control over my emotions. My heartbeat still drummed in my chest, echoing through the room. All the light in the room wasn't enough to dispel the darkness within.

The day's events that had led to this came crashing down on me. My heart contorted in pain and the lump pushed through my throat.

"We broke up." Tears burst forth, streaming down my cheeks until I had nothing left. I shared every detail with Abby, pouring out my heart because I needed to unburden myself.

"Oh, Ivy...Do you want to come back to Boston? Take some time off, maybe? It might do you good," Abby suggested. She was still in Boston, at least for now, and she and Boston had always been my safe heaven. Leaving it was a big, huge, massive mistake on my part.

I sniffled. "Yeah. The sooner I get out of this city, the better I'll be."

"You went through so much and you never thought of calling me?"

"How many times can I call you about my problems, Abby? You have your own life. You're moving. I don't expect you to be my therapist."

"I enjoy being your therapist." She attempted to lift my spirits with her cheerful tone.

And I smiled a little, even through my pain. She knew me too well. "Nick wasn't who I thought he was," I told her. "And Ryan was livid when he found out about us. I still can't figure out how I was so wrong about everything."

"Don't blame yourself. And definitely don't psychoanalyze yourself right now. The only thing you'll do is give yourself a headache. Come back to Boston so you can think straight again."

"You're right," I said, with a deep sigh. There was nothing left for me here, anyway. "I'm coming back."

"Good. And don't make any hasty decisions. Give yourself time."

That ticked me off. "Did you hear everything I said? Nick lied to me. He deceived me into moving here. He tracks my phone. He's trying to put me in shackles in the name of security. There is only one decision to make here."

"He's a real idiot if he thinks you'll accept any of that."

"Why do I sense a 'but' coming?" My left eye twitched.

"But he called me and asked me to check on you. He was worried about you, but never told me you guys broke up."

"He called you? What, you guys are friends now?" I sneered, thoroughly exasperated. And completely disregarding that he called Abby out of concern for me.

I heard her frustrated exhalation loud and clear, revealing her annoyance at my questioning her loyalty. "You're my friend, Ivy, and always will be, no matter what. This was the first time Nick called me and it was only because he was worried about you. If it bothers you, I won't pick up his calls again. I promise."

Crap! Her words made me sound so freaking foolish, like a child dictating to her friend whom she could and could not be friends with. I was clearly losing my grip. "I'm sorry. That was very immature of me. You can speak to anyone you want. I...I don't think I'll ever be able to forgive him for everything he has done."

"I get it." Abby's voice turned sympathetic. "Let your mind rest and let your heart heal. In the meantime, tell me what you're going to do so you don't get those nightmares again."

I had a few techniques I could try. Or I could run away to Boston like I had in the past.

"Maybe you should speak with your doctor?" Abby broke into my internal thoughts. "Does Ryan know about them?"

I shrugged like she could see me through the phone. "Ryan doesn't know. I've been dealing with them on my own. He has enough on his plate without worrying about me." Before Abby could start panicking, I added, "I'll go to my happy place where I used to go with my parents. And I'll start my run. If none of that works, I'll call Dr. Patrick."

"Come back to Boston and make an in-person appointment with him," Abby said, pushing further. When I agreed, she jumped to her next question. "Are you eating?"

"I'll head out for a run and eat on the way."

"Girlfriend, it's one in the morning."

"Girlfriend, I'm in New York. There's always some pizza joint or bodega open somewhere. Now go to sleep and let me live my messed-up nocturnal life until I see you again."

Chapter Sixteen

After another pain-stricken, sleepless night and a long run through the silent, shadowy streets, I returned to my empty, lifeless hotel room. It wasn't the room that lacked life; my own state of mind painted the world in shades of black and gray.

By five in the morning, I couldn't wait any longer. I messaged Gwen, telling her I couldn't work for her anymore. I pressed Send and then went into the bathroom to take a shower, letting the hot water wash over me and try to cleanse away the remnants of my restless night.

By the time I stepped out and checked my phone, Gwen's reply was waiting for me.

Come over. Let's talk. I'm in the office until lunch.

I debated with myself until I decided to meet her. Slipping into a white jumpsuit, I exited the hotel and found John outside standing next to the black SUV. Had he been there all along, or had he just arrived?

Deciding not to dwell on it, I walked past him without a

second glance and headed towards the brightly lit subway station just an intersection away.

I heard shuffling footsteps behind me before John spoke. "Miss Ivy, please get into the car."

I turned around with clenched fists. "Are you going to force me? Because swear to God, I am not getting into that car on my own."

He backed away immediately. Now I had lashed out at a person who had done nothing wrong except to work for my enemy. I needed to distance myself from anything and everything associated with Nicholas Branson.

THE DRAFTY AIR-CONDITIONED HALLS, THE LIVELY chatter, the sound of heels clicking against the polished floor... I used to be part of this exciting environment, and now I was not. It was the shortest job I'd ever had and melancholy didn't even come close to describing how I felt. All my dreams were shattered and there was nothing I could do to change my fate.

"Come in," Gwen called when I knocked on her door. Removing her white-rimmed glasses, she set them beside her keyboard. "Take a seat and tell me what's wrong."

"I'm assuming Nick updated you already." I pushed right in, not exactly in the mood for pleasantries.

"Yes. He called. And now I want to talk to you, but I won't do it with you standing."

Reluctantly, I took the first chair and got started. "There was a huge misunderstanding. I can't study here and I can't work for you, either. From changing universities to working for you and Nick's companies... I was in the dark about everything. I can't even explain how I feel about all of this."

I could barely hold back the tears that were ready to spill

any second. How had I gone so wrong with everything in my life?

"Ivy, I owe you an apology. I should've told you the truth the moment you stepped into my office the first day."

"Right. You should have. Nick shouldn't have done all these things behind my back, either. I feel betrayed by everyone. I didn't think of myself as naïve until now." Stopping momentarily before my emotions took over, I spoke again once my pain subsided. "I'll transfer back to Harvard."

"But you'll be losing months, if not a year."

"Yeah. Hopefully, I can take some classes during the winter semester. If not, I'll start next fall." The emptiness inside me churned with pain. Oh, God. What have I done? I literally ruined my career, my carefully planned life in a moment of weakness.

"You sure about that, Ivy? How about you give it a few days and think it through? Wasting one full year would be detrimental."

"I guess that's the price I pay for my ignorance," I said, keeping my voice steady. And then I thought of something else. "Did you really want me to work for you and be in your class? Or did you hire me because Nick asked? Either way I'm leaving, so please be honest."

Her expression softened as she assessed her response. The queasy feeling inside me wasn't letting me rest.

"You don't need to sugarcoat anything. I can take criticism." I waited for her answer, all the while sitting on the edge of the chair and ready to bolt if it all got too much.

"Rob and I discussed you long before Nicholas approached me. You were one of Rob's favorite students. He always said you were one of the smartest, but most directionless, student he'd ever taught."

"That doesn't sound like a compliment."

"It isn't." She chuckled to herself and continued. "Rob asked me to take you under my wing. When Nicholas came to me with his proposal, I agreed that New York City was the place where you could flourish. I'm already talking to a few companies on your behalf. They will need interns soon and they would be lucky to have you."

"I mean no disrespect, Gwen, but I don't need you to do favors for me out of guilt."

She left her chair, rounded the desk, and stood beside me. "Deceiving you wasn't my intention. I assure you I meant no harm. I don't know what happened between you and Nicholas, but I saw your potential and all I've ever wanted was for you to succeed."

I blinked back the tears. "I didn't want to work for Nick. He did all of this against my wishes."

"Work for Nick? Ivy, you work for me."

"He will be the client. Or am I wrong?" I conveyed my predicament while choking on the lump of pain. "He'll pay my salary and he'll dictate terms."

"You're bright. Don't let anything get in the way of reaching your dreams. Not even a man," she exhaled. "I'm not telling you to choose a career over everything else. But until you find what you're looking for, stick to what you're good at. Believe me, the rest will fall into place. And in case you're wondering, Nicholas never asked me to hire you. It was solely my decision."

Nick had told me the same thing, but I couldn't trust him. With the house of smoke and mirrors shattering, there was no one left for me to trust. He destroyed me in the worst possible way, leaving me questioning my capabilities. Was I ever good enough for anything significant, or had he been propping me up all along? Fooling me into believing I was capable when, in reality, I was nothing without him. God! he completely shattered my self-trust.

When I didn't respond, Gwen continued, "You're working here because I wanted you to be my assistant, and because Rob vouched for you. Besides, these projects are too exciting to pass up. Your expertise lies in business development for startups. I've kept track of all your projects over the last couple of years. Ivy, if you're one of those rich kids who enroll in university because they won't get their inheritance otherwise, don't waste my time. But if you want to make something out of yourself, then stay."

I chewed on my bottom lip, thinking hard about my next words. "I recently found out how arrogant Nick really is. To control me, he's been buying every company I work at. I'm no longer sure if I was really good at what I did or if Nick made it easier for me."

My ears burned, probably turning red with embarrassment. But noticing the shock in Gwen's eyes made me feel better. Apparently, she either didn't know how far Nick's control went or she didn't approve—or both.

"Don't lose your confidence, Ivy. You're one of the most deserving and smartest student we know."

I stayed silent because she nailed it. My confidence was shaken.

"Okay, let's break it down," she responded after a minute of silence. "Reasons aside, he buys every startup you join because he can. What are your options here?"

I shrugged, feeling emotionally drained and unable to brainstorm my next move.

"Here's how I see it—you don't work at all; or join your family business; or find a new passion; or get hired by a bigger corporation that Nick can't easily buy. Which option do you prefer?" Her words made it all too real, adding to the pain I was already feeling. Not that I hadn't thought it through, but when she said it out loud, it all became true.

"None of those options makes me happy," I finally said, tears choking me.

Gwen leaned against the desk and put a hand over my shoulder. "Makes sense. How about working as a consultant, regardless of the company or who owns it? You choose the projects you want, reject the ones you don't want, make your own rules, and stay untouchable."

That sounded better than all the other options she mentioned. Not that I had many choices left, which was my freaking dilemma.

"You're brilliant, so don't second guess yourself," her words made me marginally better, but I needed more than her words to feel confident.

When I didn't respond, Gwen offered one more option. "Stay here with me until you decide or find a suitable internship. It'll also give me time to find a replacement. Does that work for you?"

My options were limited, to say the best. I was desperate to work, both to keep my sanity and keep myself occupied. I had much to learn, and I loved the project I was working on. This job had been perfect and Nick ruined it with his selfishness—his self-centered, egotistical—

"Don't leave the MBA program. You can transfer to Harvard in a few months, but don't let an entire year go to waste because of whatever is going on in your personal life. Running away might feel like the right thing to do, but I promise you, you will regret it later."

Every part of me wanted to be as far away from here as possible, but Gwen was right. I decided to take her advice and stick it out until I figured out what I was going to do.

Indecision clouded me. After much deliberation, I gave her a reluctant nod.

I spent the rest of the day glued to my computer, trying my best to focus on my project and not on the dumpster fire that was my life.

———

AT THE END OF THE WORKDAY, I WISHED GWEN A good night and made my way to the subway station. While riding to the hotel, I decided to take a brief detour.

Revisiting Bethesda Terrace after a decade felt like a journey through time. Familiar sights and the intricately designed architecture stirred up a rush of nostalgia. Once-familiar steps felt different today, evoking memories lost in the past. The significance of this place remained despite how much time had gone by.

Kids ran around splashing in the fountain, lovers sat on benches stealing kisses, and families set up picnic blankets. Every single person around me seemed happy.

Forgetting my inner turmoil, I tried to find happiness in every little thing Central Park offered. A memory stuck in time surfaced, my mother's beautiful face. Sometimes reflected in my mirror. Her laughter at every small thing we shared. Her soft fingers holding my hand. Time stood still as I remembered those sensations. The sentimental value of those moments we spent together outweighed the inheritance they left behind.

I wandered, listening to street musicians sing and play their instruments. The city had changed little, but the art had evolved. Today, a band was playing instruments on their iPads while a woman danced flamenco in black.

A soap bubble floated to me and popped when it touched my nose, making the soap particles tickle my face. Leaving the upbeat crowd, I joined a group of kids and chased after the bubbles with them. I laughed when they giggled, after what felt like ages.

"You look beautiful when you laugh, sweetheart."

Nick's voice made me stop and turn.

Disregarding how my heart raced from his sheer presence, I snapped. "Are you still following me?"

"I'm not. I'm here and you're here, that's all." Straightening his tie, he moved a step closer. His vest and jacket were gone and his shirtsleeves were rolled up to his elbows. Effortlessly, he drew me into his cosmos again. I hated how my heart flipped every time we were near each other. "I know you came here often with your mother. It was your favorite place to talk things out and reconcile."

I looked at him in utter disbelief. Shocked. No one knew that except my mother and me and... "How do you remember that? I only told you once, many years ago."

"In two nights and one whole day, from your earliest memories to the day of the accident... I never forget anything you tell me, Ivy."

My heart somersaulted under my chest. I didn't want to fall for his sweet words again, so I masked my feelings with irritation. "You said you would never come back, yet here you are. Was that another one of your lies?"

His smile left his face. My heart was gutted raw.

"Use the car, baby."

Ignoring him, as well as my feelings for him, I started walking up the grand stairs. Nick joined me there as well. "When I hide the truth, you call me controlling. When I tell you the truth, you break up with me. How will we ever move forward if I don't understand what you want?"

I didn't know how to make him understand that being

truthful and non-controlling had to come naturally into a relationship. It wasn't something I could teach or explain.

"Come home, sweetheart."

"Stop. Calling me. That." I closed my eyes, hoping that if I didn't see him, he wouldn't exist—that my feelings for him would somehow vanish, and I would be over my heartache.

When I opened my eyes, he was still clenching his fists and mirroring my exasperation. "Let John take you wherever you need to go."

I fixed him with an icy stare. Our eyes locked in the silent battle of wills.

"I would rather die than sit in your car." I reestablished my position. "We are done, Nick. Over. Finished."

He slid one hand around my waist and pulled me closer, making my entire life condense into this singular moment. My heart raced, his breathing got shallow, and soon we were breathing each other's air. How we went from cold to hot in a nano-second was hard to comprehend. No matter how much I tried to be upset, all I saw in his eyes was immense love for me.

Passersby paused briefly, casting a quick glance before continuing on their way. "Someone might take pictures of us," I whispered.

"I don't care," he replied.

"Ryan will be upset," I said, hoping to sway him.

"Right now, I don't care about that either," he responded dismissively.

"You told me you never pursued me," I said, confronting him about his previous statement when we first met here.

"I wasn't completely honest," he confessed. "There was not a single day that I didn't think about you."

I remained there, feeling safe and content in his arms and feeling his shallow heartbeat beneath the palm of my hand.

An audible whisper spread over my skin when his lips touched mine. "Tell me you don't want to be with me."

"At what cost, Nick?" I held back my tears.

"Tell me your feelings have changed and I'll leave."

From deep feelings I never labeled, to longing, to heartbreak and every emotional rollercoaster in between, I averted gaze to conceal my emotions. Once again, the pain was searing as I failed to reach him. It seemed impossible to make him understand the magnitude of his actions. The deceit... the manipulation that consumed my existence... I couldn't accept any of it. Yet I couldn't bear the thought of a life without Nick, either.

Tears welled in my eyes. He was my lifeline. His arms surrounded me. Yet the river that ran between us was too wide and treacherous to cross.

"It breaks my heart to see you like this. I thought you would be happy here, with me," Nick whispered. His other hand moved to my back, covering me, protecting me, trying to prove what this feeling meant.

Wrapped in his arms, where I was always the most fulfilled and happy, I struggled with conflicting feelings of contentment and independence. My heart reminded me this was exactly where I wanted to be. My rational mind said I couldn't let him run my life and dictate the terms of our relationship.

My heart pleaded to surrender completely. My mind told me not to lose self-respect. My heart begged me to find a middle ground. My mind told me I would lose my identity. Trust, respect, support, love, dreams, desire, want, and need—I wanted everything from him. With him.

"Your presence hurts me, Nick." Tears rolled down my cheeks. There was no stopping them. "I don't want to be with you."

His hands fell away. His eyes were filled with the same hurt that lived in my heart. It was impossible not to love Nick, for he was a part of me… he was my heart, my soul, my everything. And yet, I couldn't go on this way. Lies. Deceit. Betrayal. He shattered me to pieces.

"If you really want me to be happy, you will honor your word and never contact me again."

I ran off, carrying my broken heart beneath my chest. And I didn't look back.

Chapter Seventeen

"What are you doing up so late?"

Nick's deep voice startled me, making me jump. The photo slipped from my hand, landing near my feet. Instead of rising from the stool to pick it up, I tugged at my cotton sleeve to wipe away the tears.

I sensed him moving closer, so close that his arm slightly brushed against my hipbone and then my leg. It wasn't intentional, but I was aware of his every movement. He bent down to retrieve the photo, then hesitated, standing still, before he picked it up and turned to me. I couldn't bring myself to speak. The ache in my chest was still too raw, threatening to overwhelm me.

"Ivy, are you... all right?" Nick gently wrapped an arm around my shoulders and pulled me into his warmth. "Do you want to talk about it?"

I shook my head and took the photo of my parents from his hand, tucking it between the pages of the book I had been trying to read for the last thirty minutes. My nightmare had shaken me awake. Trying to get rid of the residual grief, I'd grabbed my *book and come down to the kitchen, confident everyone would be asleep at this time of the night. But Nick found me. He always did.*

"What are you doing up so late?" I finally managed to ask when I found my voice again. I didn't want to come across as an emotional wreck. Ryan, his friends, and their families were all I had left. I didn't want to be a burden or make them feel like I needed more than they were already offering.

"Your nocturnal tendencies aren't exactly a secret to me. Talk to me, Ivy," Nick urged, his voice tinged with genuine concern.

The lump of pain returned, and I couldn't speak. I missed my parents—madly. Every waking moment reminded me of the life I could have had if they were still alive. Every night, I relived the horror of losing everything in the blink of an eye.

Nick turned me to face him, pulling up a stool so he could sit in front of me. We were at the kitchen island with the bright glow of the light illuminating every surface, casting lines over his face, making him more striking.

I dabbed at my eyes, struggling to find my voice. "I'm sorry."

"For what? Missing your parents? You don't have to apologize for anything, Ivy." He cupped my face in his hands, forcing me to meet his gaze. His eyes were soft, gentle, as if he were relieved to have found me. "If I could bring them back, believe me, I would. Seeing you sad hits me in the gut every time."

I absorbed his words, but I didn't know what to say. This infatuation of mine was turning into love with every passing day.

"Never forget that my parents love you as much as they love me. You can call them anytime, you know? You don't have to wait for the holidays to visit."

I nodded.

"What happened to you and Ryan was tragic," he said. "It

might feel impossible now, but you're stronger than you think. One day you'll get over the pain. Trust me."

"I'm not strong by any mean." And I doubted getting past this ordeal. Ever. I replied in a low voice, "I'll never forget my parents."

"And you shouldn't. They were amazing people who raised incredible kids. I'll forever be grateful to them—for giving me my best friend, and..."

He trailed off, his words hanging in the air. Unfinished. Did he want to say something about me? Did I mean something to him? Should I ask him to continue or leave it be? Our gaze stayed locked, but I couldn't read his thoughts. Suddenly, my grief faded, replaced by a singular awareness of him. Nick. His presence when I was lonely. His words that filled the cracks in my heart.

His hands slid from my face to my shoulders, then down my arms, until he clasped my hands in his. He smiled, taking my breath away. "Can I tell you a secret?"

"Yes." I smiled back, trying to shake off my embarrassment and trying to hide my feelings for him.

"Before I picked up that photo, my heart pounded, thinking it might be a picture of your boyfriend or some guy you like." Damn, if he tried to distract me from my previous thoughts, it worked.

"I don't have a boyfriend," I replied, seriously. Incredulously.

"Never or now?" he asked, teasing.

"Never. No boyfriend ever." What I wanted to say was I wished he could be the first. The words sat on the tip of my tongue, but never uttered.

"Good. How old are you anyway, ten?" He turned serious in a blink of an eye. "Focus on your studies, you're too young."

I rolled my eyes and got up from my seat. I knew he was trying to distract me from thoughts of my parents, but the subject of boyfriends was sensitive, especially coming from him. "I'm turning sixteen next week," I said proudly, as if it were one of my greatest accomplishments.

He laughed wretchedly.

I pulled my hand from his and took a step away from the island. My mind screamed with the question I wanted him to ask: Ask me! Ask me to be your girlfriend. Because I so desperately want you to be my boyfriend.

Nick caught my hand and turned me back to face him. The rub of his thumb against my fingers was raising waves inside my belly. Butterflies flying high from my diaphragm to my chest. Knocking down dizzy, getting up and flying back again. If he would not make the move, could I? Should I kiss him?

"You're still a child." As if reading my mind, Nick said to keep those thoughts at bay.

"I've got too many guardians." Frustrated, I raised a brow. Trying to bait him, hoping he'd see me as more than just a kid. I knew his feelings for me were different from what Ryan or his other friends had. Deeper as well, because these special moments we had now and then were something I knew he cherished. There was a lot more between us, yet he was always holding back.

Nick didn't pull me closer, didn't kiss me, or hug me, even though I stood between his legs. His gaze locked on mine, his jaw hard, always careful not to cross any line. "Guardian or not, I'll always protect you, Ivy, because you're Ryan's sister. Tell me about your holidays when your parents were alive."

And... he changed the subject, putting me in my place again. Keeping our attraction aside, he reminded me of the only relationship we had. He was my brother's best friend, and I was his best friend's sister. Only thing he delved into were things that bothered me.

"Why do you want to know?" I asked, my voice barely a

whisper from my rising desires, totally unaffected by his brush off.

His response was immediate, always trying to break the spell between us and forcing me to focus on his words. "Because I want to know everything about you. And because I want you to remember the good times you shared with them."

Monday turned into Thursday. At last I was moving into my new apartment on the Upper West Side, away from Nick and Ryan, and closer to the university.

I needed my space. I did better when I was alone. Ryan was speaking to me again, and had helped me find an apartment in one of McAlister's buildings. A heavily guarded building I cared nothing about, but I would do anything to be in my brother's good books.

Ryan and I met every day, but we never spoke about Nick. Whether they were still friends or were at odds, I couldn't tell. It was a topic we both avoided at all costs.

Abby checked in on me every morning to make sure I had nightmare-free sleep. If she was in touch with Nick, she didn't mention it and I didn't ask. After that awful night at the hotel, I had a few more episodes. It was the same dream repeating itself, but it always faded away when Nick called my name. Even when we were apart, his endearing voice had the power to pull me out of those dreadful ordeals.

The distance between us started killing me slowly. But I didn't know how to be with him and not get hurt. He was my poison and antidote, all wrapped in one. My heart was constantly at war with itself.

What I wanted and what I had was a contrast. I wanted Nick. I was forlorn.

I resumed using public transportation and went running every time I missed Nick, which was almost all the time. I kept myself occupied with work and surrounded myself with friends. Whenever I had a free evening, I filled it with any activity I could find so I didn't have time to wallow in my despair.

Since I hadn't brought anything from Boston, I had to buy new furniture for my apartment. Risha helped with everything and made the place feel like home. Apparently, interior design was one of her hobbies. I loved spending time with her and she helped me decorate. It was a win-win.

John was always on my tail. After the hotel incident, he never asked me to get into the car, but he stayed close all the time. When I took the subway, he came on foot. When I asked why he was following me, he told me it was a big city, and he couldn't help it if I went to the same places as he did. I gave up, ignoring his presence as best I could.

Pictures of me and Nick in the park never made it to the news. As far as the paparazzi and the journalists could tell, we were over. I took Rachael's advice and put two Google alerts on my phone: one for Nick and one for myself. I knew I would be miserable seeing pictures of him, but I was hurting and I wanted to know what he was doing, and if he was as wounded as I was. If he was missing me the way I missed him.

It turned out that Nick had moved on with his life faster than I'd anticipated. Within twenty-four hours, he was with someone else. Seeing him with another woman wrecked me. I wasn't expecting him to forget me so fast—but then again, what *was* I expecting? I had told him to leave, and he left.

Seeing him with the same woman every day satisfied the media and took the attention off of me. I should've been happy, but there was no gaiety without Nick.

———

"So, how does it feel to live on your own?" Rachael asked as we settled on the couch with martini glasses in hand. It was Friday evening, and Dustin and Rachael had come over to my new apartment to give me company and make sure I wasn't lonely.

I'd gotten what I said I wanted—living alone and experiencing the city on my own—yet it was doing nothing to make me feel any better about my decision.

Everything reminded me of Nick. Even the act of moving to a new apartment made me think of him. In a perfect world, Nick and I would've been together. We would be sitting here watching the soccer game. USA was playing Spain tonight and losing yet again.

I knew Nick wouldn't miss the game. I couldn't help but wonder who he was watching it with, or if he was watching the game with *her* as well—Sylvie Russo, the woman that the paparazzi couldn't stop talking about. Bold and independent, she wanted to be the one who stopped Nicholas Branson from wandering around. *If she's so independent, I'd like to see Nick try to control her the way he did me.* My thoughts were bitter, unwarranted. I needed to stop thinking about them.

"I'm looking forward to my first night in my new apartment," I said, snapping out of my thoughts and muting the game. Without Nick, soccer didn't hold the same excitement. I only watched it to feel connected to him in some way. "Rachael, how's it going with Chiq Boutique? Are you making progress?"

"Ugh!" she grunted out loud. "Don't even ask. It's exhausting. I don't even remember the last time I sketched a new dress design. I'm supposed to be a fashion designer, not an architect, interior designer, accountant, and marketing specialist, all rolled into one."

Dustin laughed. I did, too. Rachael entertained us with

more stories about getting her boutique store off the ground. As awful as she said things were going, there was one thing we knew for sure: Chiq was going to be the talk of the town as soon as it opened its doors.

"Thanks for coming over," I said. "It was sweet of you guys."

"We love hanging out with you. Though I have to say, Friday nights are better enjoyed at a nightclub instead of an apartment," Dustin said. "That, and watching soccer on mute."

"What are you complaining about?" I threw a bold flowered decorative cushion at him. "The last time I checked, no one forced you to come today." He canceled his previous plans to be here, even though I told him not to.

"No one, except you. You begged me to join you girls. 'Please come *over*, Dustin. It's so *boring* without you, Dustin!'" Mocking my voice, he got on his knees in front of me with his hands folded in a prayer-like gesture.

"I guess all the acting classes your parents made you take are finally paying off," I teased, and threw another cushion at him.

For the next hour, we laughed, made fun of each other, and tried to get into the groove of being friends. Once again, it felt like old times.

"You should laugh more often. It suits you, Ivy." Rachael's words made me pause, reminding me of how Nick told me something similar when we last met. "And learn to ignore gossip."

She held out her phone for me. An hour-old story about Nick's company being under investigation filled the screen.

My heart sank. I read the story in its entirety, but it revealed little. Thankfully, the stocks were still soaring high after Nick's short and powerful statement.

"Branson Capital is fully cooperating with all audit demands. Transparency is our top priority. We have nothing to hide."

I watched the video thrice on repeat. Seeing him wasn't easy, and I missed him miserably all the time. I was still breathing and doing everything I was expected to do, but I had stopped living the day we broke up. I was good at pretending.

"Did he try to make things right between you?" Rachael asked before I could hit the play button for the fourth time.

"Nope. After the park incident he never came after me, Rach. We're over." I returned her phone, tucked my feet under me, and sipped my cocktail. I tried to sound strong, like I was determined to get over the failed relationship.

It's not possible and you know that.

"He didn't deserve you. It's good that you didn't waste your time on him." Dustin couldn't hide his disdain for Nick.

"Someone is passing judgment here." Rachael gave Dustin a back-off look.

He definitely didn't get the hint. "I just don't like how he treated Ivy, that's all."

Rachael looked at me, staying mute. She knew my feelings for Nick were deeper and meant more than any fight. Even another woman in his life couldn't make me feel any different.

"So, did anyone get an invitation to The Gotham Ball next Sunday?" Dustin decided to change the course of our discussion, which was probably for the best.

"A genuine invitation? I got it yesterday and thought it was junk mail," I said.

Rachael's mouth flew open in a very dramatic way. "Don't tell me you threw it out!"

I fished it out of a drawer and dropped it in her lap. She breathed a mocking sigh of relief. The drama.

"Woman, you need to stay up to date if you want to survive

in Manhattan," Dustin exclaimed. "Gotham Ball is one of the most sought-after events of the summer. If you get an invitation, it means you are the crème de la crème of high society."

"In that case, they definitely made a mistake. I just moved back. Barely anyone knows me here. There is no reason they would send me an invitation," I said, shrugging.

"Exactly! You're a perfect mystery. That's why everybody wants to know who this Ivy McAlister really is. But once they meet you and find out how boring you are, they'll start ignoring you." Dustin made a smug face and threw a pillow back at me.

Rachael gave Dustin a playful nudge. "You're the rich girl who ran away, snagged one of the most eligible bachelors the moment you returned, who is also your brother's best friend. That's why all the gossip magazines and socialites are so curious about you."

Was I supposed to feel better about the unsettling explanation behind getting the invitation? "It doesn't matter. I'm not going," I announced, which earned me some downright horrified eye rolls from Rachael.

"Are you crazy?" Dustin sat up straight.

Rachael nodded in agreement. "You have to go. It's the event of the social season!"

They couldn't stop there, deciding to give me a crash course on all the important events and dinners I had to attend to make connections and be someone in this city.

I didn't want to be anyone in the city. I liked being anonymous.

After my *Party Guide for Dummies* course, Rachael called a cab. We said our goodbyes and sent her home. I switched off the TV—the US team had lost again—and walked with Dustin out to his car.

Just then, a message from Risha popped up in a group chat we shared with Cece. ***Dinner tomorrow?***

Cece didn't waste any time joining in. ***Reynold will join us. Can you ask Ryan as well?***

I turned to Dustin, who was getting into the car. "Any plans for tomorrow evening?"

"Nothing in particular. What do you have in mind?"

"Ryan, Risha, Cece, Reynold, and I are meeting for dinner. Want to come? It's not a couple's dinner, I promise," I quickly added. "I don't want to go alone. Absolutely no pressure though," I was babbling now, wanting to make sure he didn't come to any wrong conclusions.

"You know you can ask without overthinking, right? That's what friends are for."

Chapter Eighteen

Saturday morning, I woke up to multiple Google alerts. First was a picture of Dustin and me standing near his car last night. I had a massive smile on my face—because he had just agreed for the dinner. *"Finally! Some happiness in Ivy McAlister's life!"* the caption screamed.

Could these gossip rags be any more infuriating?

Irritated, I deleted the alert and went to the next one. It was Nick with Sylvie Russo at a dinner event, and he was pulling a chair out for her. His one hand rested on her back, disappearing beyond her shoulder. From the angle of the photograph I couldn't see the back of her dress, but I desperately hoped it was as modest as the front. The crimson satin hugged her bosom and clung to her every perfect curve. Her self-assured smile, haloed by her yellowish blonde cascading hair, radiated confidence. Expressive eyes locked on Nick's, mixed with a hint of desire and the subtleness of love.

The aggravating caption read, *"Nicholas Branson, ladies' man, has finally found his match."*

I burned with jealousy. And I hated her.

———

LATER THAT EVENING, I ENTERED AN ULTRA-CHIC French fusion restaurant that had recently opened in Tribeca. In a gray blazer and jeans, Ryan was stealing the show. Every woman's eyes were on him, but as usual, he didn't glance at a single woman here. Unlike Nick, Ryan was completely committed to his relationship. It made me wonder how they had become best friends in the first place when they were so different. And could that be the reason Ryan was so against this relationship?

Risha and Cece were busy catching up. Dustin and Reynold were chatting over a glass of whiskey, which left Ryan and me to spend some time by ourselves. He got up from his chair and asked me to join him at the bar for some brother-sister time.

"Good to see you're moving on, Ivy." Ryan turned to the bartender and ordered our drinks.

I immediately regretted my decision to invite Dustin tonight. "He's just a friend, Ryan."

"I hope you weren't serious about Nick. I would never forgive myself if you left New York because of him."

He was regretting his decision to let Nick watch over me—to take me places when I first got back. The truth was far from it. Nick and I somehow would've found our way to each other. From chemistry to our deep feelings, everything between us was too strong to be contained, to avoid or ignore.

"Whatever it was, it's over now. Please don't blame yourself for any of it. Regarding staying or leaving the city, I'm not sure if I want this unnecessary media attention. This life was never for me, Ryan." Being honest felt good, too.

"I know, and that's my fear too." He didn't elaborate, but his concern, as always, was evident. In many ways, he tried to be my parent and my brother all wrapped into one.

I touched his arm reassuringly. "For now, I'm not going anywhere. I'll keep a low profile and the paparazzi will get bored with me soon. It's not like I'm a celebrity or anything."

He chuckled slightly. "No, you're not. You just got involved with the wrong guy at the wrong time."

"And I'm really sorry for coming between you two. I don't know what I was thinking."

"Nick should've known better," Ryan said. "He betrayed my trust."

"So did I, Ryan." I had hurt the only family I had, and now Ryan would always blame himself for my bad choices. "Are you in touch with him?"

"Our friendship ended the day he went after you."

That broke my heart. Years of friendship destroyed in a few weeks, and it was all because of me. Since this was the first time Ryan and I had spoken about Nick, I tried to get him to open up a little. "Why were you so against Nick and me dating anyway? Is he that bad?"

"No. He would do anything for the people he loves." Ryan took a sip of his drink before continuing, "His problem is he loves very few people in his life. And those he doesn't love, he couldn't care less if they live or die."

"So, he lacks compassion?" I tried to understand the man who never left my heart.

Ryan gave it some thought before responding. "His relationships with women have been questionable at best. The guy is a commitment phobe and he doesn't care what happens to the women he leaves behind."

A commitment-phobic man who wanted me to move in?

"He never loved anyone?" I asked, hope blooming in my heart against my better judgement.

"Or respected. Or trusted," Ryan stated.

"You do know I trust Nick with my life, right? He didn't care about himself when I got into that bike accident. He saved my life that day, risking his own."

"That was a lifetime ago. He's changed since then. Trust me, Ivy, you are better off without him."

"When did he change? Because the man I knew and the one you're describing aren't the same." I pushed further.

"He doesn't talk about what, how, when... but something inside him snapped turning him into a cold, heartless man."

Ryan's words weren't convincing enough, but there was definitely more to Nick than I knew. I still couldn't imagine him hurting me. Then. Or now.

But he has hurt you, Ivy. Emotionally. He lied to you. And he has never apologized for anything he has done.

"Nick is a very self-centered man, and I know that because I'm his closest friend." Ryan broke into my thoughts.

Not wanting to delve further, I swiftly changed the topic. "The investigation his company is going through, how serious is it?"

"It's serious enough. And it's only the beginning," he muttered, fixating on his drink. My brother, just as concerned as I was, couldn't hide his worry. I also knew Ryan well enough that he would never assist Nick, as I was his primary responsibility.

But this new piece of information didn't sit too well. I was reading every news article out there and they all said very little about the facts and speculated more. "How did he get mixed up in something like that?"

"On his obsession to be at the top, he made a lot of enemies. I'm sure one of them is coming after him now."

Was that the reason for the slashed tires? Is that why he was so set on protecting me?

I had too many questions, and Ryan was responding. I decided to take advantage and went on. "Has Nick been involved in something illegal?"

His dry laugh brought my thoughts to a halt. "Nick is an honest businessman, Ivy. He has a drive that none of us possess. We dream. He turns them into reality. I wouldn't doubt his business ethics, but his fixation on dominating everything he touches is unsettling."

A man of his power and stature, accustomed to being in control, must be feeling powerless under these circumstances. I couldn't imagine what he was going through. "Can he get out of this mess on his own?" I asked.

Ryan looked sideways, giving me a disapproving glance. "I can see what you're thinking. Stay away from him, Ivy. You're too young to know how his mind works. Nick is a shrewd businessman who knows how to handle his problems. He doesn't need anyone. And you are not cut out for that kind of life."

His eyes didn't leave my face until I gave a nod of acknowledgement.

"One last thing," I quickly asked before my window of opportunity closed. "What happens to all the joint ventures?" I knew this was a significant part of our hospitality business. Branson Capital could handle the pressure, but I had my reservations about the McAlister Group.

"Leave that to me. Now, let's go. Everybody is waiting for us." And just like that, Ryan switched off on the line of conversation I had pursued. We headed to our table, where I greeted my friends, and we all sat down, eager to order.

The rest of our dinner was pleasant. We drank some of the finest wine and ate the best boeuf bourguignon the city had to offer. I laughed with everyone to show I was okay. We joked around, and made Reynold feel included.

Dustin was amazing. I was under his friendly, watchful eyes the entire evening. In some ways, he reminded me of Mike.

Icy shivers went down my spine, remembering the mess I had left behind in Boston.

———

"I'm heading to Paris tomorrow," Dustin decided to mention his upcoming trip that he told me a few times already. "Don't you dare party too hard until I return."

"Say hello to your parents when you see them. And... I'm sorry about all the rumors circulating about you and me." We were driving back from the restaurant when I apologized. None of it was my fault, and yet it was. If I wasn't involved with Nick, no one would have glanced at me.

It was bad enough that I was Nicholas Branson's ex. Now the rumor that I was with Dustin Hart was circulating. From friends to lovers, our relationship was "strong", according to the media. Where they got all the make-believe scoop was still a mystery to me.

"I can't complain. Dad said our business is booming because of Hart Industries being in the news." He laughed at his own joke.

Hart Industries manufactured specialized products for airplanes. I was pretty sure his statement was completely baseless. The company was doing well regardless of the press or our supposed relationship.

"But seriously, don't read too much into these gossip columns." Dustin took a right to exit the Columbus Circle. "They sensationalize everything in order to sell their paper."

"Glad you think that way." I rested my head on the glass

pane and closed my eyes. Rewinding and replaying Ryan and my conversation in my head. "I hate to be part of it. The sooner they get out of my hair, the better I'll be."

"I'm happy to see that you're over that douchebag. Flings like that usually end in heartbreak. Not worth it."

What's with these two men and their dislike for each other? I refrained from correcting Dustin. My reason for our breakup could be anything, but Nick being an insensitive, unsympathetic douchebag wasn't one of them.

"Speaking of flings and heartbreaks, is there anyone special in your life?" I shifted the spotlight onto him instead.

"Nobody special at the moment."

"A recent breakup, then?" I pushed further.

"She asked me if I loved her and I couldn't lie." He started fidgeting with the car radio, which was already playing his favorite jazz. Clearly, he was mending his broken heart and wasn't ready to share more than he already had. I changed the direction of our discussion to lighter topics, so he didn't feel obligated to give me more details.

I knew the feeling well. The pain I carried in my heart traveled everywhere I went. I pretended to be happy; I laughed; and I spent time with my friends and my family. But inside, I was in constant agony. The pain was part of me and always waiting to swallow me.

This wasn't a battle I could win, because the only one I was fighting was myself.

———

As soon as I got home and removed my cell phone from my purse, I got Noah's voicemail. There was to be a birthday bash tomorrow night at the brand-new Tao nightclub in Midtown. A VIP table had been reserved, and my presence was mandatory.

I went from a lazy Sunday to having to put together a party outfit in less than twenty-four hours. After my run, I took a shower and got into bed. Before I shut off the lights, my phone pinged. Nick hadn't texted me in a week but for whatever reason, he had decided tonight of all nights to break his streak.

Stay home.

Chapter Nineteen

Another sleepless night came and went. My weekend was a series of get-togethers to keep me sane. I had no reason to follow Nick's orders when he had been ignoring me and had obviously moved on with his own life.

Nowadays, I needed little persuasion to do things and go places. If I got an invitation, I went. Anything was better than a lonely apartment and a tear-stained pillow.

I got off the cab in front of Tao. The sheer number of people outside the club astonished me. This city was always celebrating something. Rachael was right; if someone was lonely in New York City, it wasn't the city's fault. So here I was once again, trying to find a place for myself.

Noah removed his VIP card from the inside of his jacket. The bouncer moved left, giving us space to get in, and Rachel, Noah, and I headed down the long, red corridor of the club.

Loud hip-hop music, people grinding on each other on the dance floor—this place was *happening*. We got seated at a reserved table in the corner. Since the rest of Noah's friends weren't here yet, we ordered a round of drinks for ourselves.

I opened my purse, looking for my driver's license, when I got another text.

Go home.

My heart raced at a million beats per second. My eyes immediately scanned the place as far as it could travel. Unfortunately, I couldn't see too far, thanks to the annoying artificial smoke that was coming in through the floor. The anticipation of potentially getting to see Nick in person awakened the butterflies in my stomach, the diminutive insects whose survival was dependent on Nick.

A loud popping sound brought me back to the present. Noah opened the bottle of champagne and let the bubbly liquid spill onto the floor. Pushing Nick out of my head, I put my phone into the side pocket of my skirt and joined the celebration.

Cece and Risha took it upon themselves to dress me up with absolutely no regard for my comfort. Two knots held my backless top in place, one on my neck and one in the center of my back. Years ago, the money I'd spent on the top seemed like a great purchase—but not so much when I wore it tonight. It elevated sexiness to the next level and that, for sure, wasn't my style.

I also wore a short leather skirt and red high-heeled boots. The girls used the words "sizzling hot." They wanted me to forget Nick and have fun tonight, not saying it to my face, but I read between the lines.

I was putting my champagne flute down on the table when I noticed a familiar face in my peripheral vision. Excusing myself, I went after the man. "Taber, hi! What a coincidence."

Friends since their undergrad days—Nick, Jonah, Ryan, and Taber—had been inseparable ever since. It wasn't just the guys; all the families had maintained close relationships and business partnerships over the years. Cece, being Taber's sister and my close friend, was another angle to our relationship.

A broad smile lit up Taber's face as soon as he saw me. "Coincidence, indeed. How have you been?"

"Couldn't be better." I walked with him to my table. "Let me guess. You own this club?"

"You guessed right. I opened it a month ago. That's why you found me here."

"I was going to ask what an old-timer like you is doing at the club," I teased him, remembering our last conversation at Nick's parents' house.

"Oh, please. Your generation needs some serious dancing and drinking lessons. You're at my club to get an education no school can provide."

Our banter continued until Noah's friends started showing up one by one.

"Let me know if you guys want to move to the VVIP lounge on the third floor," Taber told us, once the initial introductions were done, and everybody's face lit up. I assumed it wasn't an easy thing to get in.

He was calling the server over before anyone had a chance to respond. Then he looked up at the reflective black glass partitions on the top floor and at the smoke and laser lights on the second.

"Just making sure the place exceeds your expectations," he said, as soon as our eyes met. There was a hint of concern, and I couldn't figure out why.

"O... kay!" I pointed my fingers at the windows. "What's behind those glass walls? Your office?"

"It's not for you." Taber started walking away. "Have a good time with your friends."

———

We decided to spend an hour at our table before heading to the exclusive VIP lounge on the third floor. As I was taking a fresh glass of champagne off of the server's tray, someone tapped my bare shoulder. I turned. "Damien?"

I let him hug me even though this was our second meeting and the first in an informal setting. I didn't mind a casual hug from a friendly, sophisticated guy.

"Never in a million years did I think I'd see you here." Damien gave me one of his charming smiles.

"I don't just work, you know. I hang out with my friends too. It's called balance."

We both laughed. The man was beyond gorgeous, attracting a lot of female attention not just in the club overall, but at our table as well. "Are you here with your friends?" I asked him, ignoring Noah's female friends.

He chuckled. "Too old to be hanging out at nightclubs now. I was upstairs with some partners when I thought I saw you. Just came down to make sure my eyes weren't playing tricks on me."

"I see." He didn't look old, late twenties at the most.

He put his hand out. "A dance?"

Instinctively, I turned to Rachael.

"You're here to have fun," she said, playfully nudging me. "Here's your chance!"

I figured I needed another sip of champagne—some much-needed liquid courage to dance with an almost stranger—when my phone vibrated in my pocket.

Stay away from Damien.

If I had any lingering doubts, they vanished immediately. He was here, watching me.

Some nerve though! The man who was having the time of his life had the audacity to tell me what to do. **I can do whatever I want, with whomever I want.**

I put my phone back in my pocket and let Damian take me to the dance floor. My phone vibrated a second time, and then a third and a fourth. I didn't bother to check it anymore.

Four years with Abby had provided plenty of exposure to nightclub dancing. Invigorating music, an excellent partner, fun people around—finally, I was letting go of my inhibitions.

Damian put his hands on my waist, and our bodies moved in sync with the music. Sometimes his hands were on my back. Sometimes my back was against his chest. Our fingers entwined and once his cheek caressed mine. He was hot, beyond attractive, with some impressive dance moves.

But he wasn't Nick.

Butterflies didn't flutter in my belly. My heart didn't skip a beat. He even had the same eyes as Nick's, but they didn't have the magnetic pull. Damien did nothing to help me forget about Nick.

Once again disappointed, I continued dancing like so many other people on the floor, resigning myself to the fact that no one in the world could replace Nick.

"You do know how to have fun. I stand corrected." Damien's voice was close to my ear.

From his lopsided smile to a glint in his eyes, he was clearly flirting with me. Before I could flirt back, my phone vibrated again.

Annoyed, I tried ignoring it, but it was impossible. I removed the phone from my pocket and saw thirty missed calls —all of them from the same number.

Damien came closer and spoke over the sound of the music. "Distracted by your phone?"

It started ringing again.

I sighed. "Sorry. I have to take this. It'll only be a minute."

"Sure, no problem."

I picked up before it went to voicemail.

"Hello—"

"Meet me at the VIP lounge on the third floor. Right. Now," Nick barked his order. Livid. Enraged.

"Listen—" The call disconnected. Great!

Telling Damien I'd be back soon, I left the dance floor. I was tipsy; I was aroused, and I wanted to see Nick in person. He was the only man my heart desired, and the only man I was furiously angry with.

———

THE DIM LIGHTS, SEDUCTIVE MUSIC, BOLD RED AND yellow couches paired with oversized chairs on brass legs made the VIP lounge look straight out of a vintage fashion magazine. Champagne bottles and gold-rimmed crystal glasses on every table, and the entire place screamed style, class, and exclusivity.

I walked past a couple who were way into their make-out session. Another booth was draped in gold beads, making it difficult to see what was happening inside. Before I peeked, someone pulled me to one side and into a room.

A door clicked and locked.

My heart did a full somersault the moment my eyes met Nick's. I sucked in a breath from the rush of adrenaline. His powerful magnetic pull surged through my veins, making it impossible to maintain the distance between us, making it impossible to breathe.

I took a step back to steady myself, and then another, until my back hit the tinted glass behind me. Standing still, I took him in. My heart was ready to jump towards him the moment he called out for me.

He didn't say anything.

In his black shirt and tailored sharkskin trousers, he looked like sin personified. His eyes held an intense, hypnotic allure that pulled me into his realm. His lips were rigid. Was he angry, perhaps?

"Is *she* here as well?" Sarcasm got the best of me. I hated her even though I had no claim on him.

"Stay away from Damien." His snide tone, jaw clenched with frustration, didn't go unnoticed.

Was he seriously angry? With me? "You can be with Sylvie Russo every day, but I can't dance with a guy one night? You haven't changed at all, have you?"

"What do you want, Ivy?"

Nothing he did or said was remotely sensual, yet the intensity in his eyes wasn't letting me breathe. My body hummed with excitement for God knew what, because he didn't take a single step towards me.

Infuriated beyond words, I challenged him. "You really want to know?"

"I'm listening."

His arrogance tipped me over. "Fine. I have my needs too. Only this time, I'm prepared to protect my heart. From now on, there will be no strings attached." I tried hard to hate him and failed miserably.

"That's it? You want to fuck someone?" he sneered in disgust.

"Yes. I do." I responded in the same tone. "I want to fuck someone. To use somebody for my pleasure and then leave as if he means nothing to me." I wanted to hurt Nick as much as he had hurt me. To break his arrogance and bring him down to his knees.

"I'm here, Ivy. Use me." His voice suddenly calmed, and he stood there with open arms, surrendering to me.

And he was mistaken if he thought I wouldn't. I ran to Nick and went straight for his shirt buttons. He folded me into his arms. I was desperate to feel him and touch every inch of him. He was my lifeline.

Tonight, I wanted to live.

My attention turned to the couch on my left. Was this a place for dark tastes? Was that why Taber told me to stay away from these rooms?

Nick bent down to kiss me. I turned. The kiss fell on my ear. He grunted in disapproval. Pushing him down onto the leather couches, I went for his zipper.

"Ivy," Nick growled, pulling me over him. His hands unfastened the knots holding my top together.

Without waiting for my permission, Nick dove for my breasts. He forced himself to be gentle, restraining from going wild. Pain shot through my nipples as soon as his lips caressed one at a time. His mouth started sucking them greedily. I sucked in my breath, breathing in his scent. Goosebumps scattered all over my skin.

I was alive again.

My hands ran over his bare torso, trying to touch and feel everything I could. Nick's possessive hold wrapped me into him, pulling me closer and wanting to end the gap between us.

Did he miss me as much as I missed him?

I unzipped his pants and pushed them down along with his boxer briefs. Glistening with pre-cum, his erection curved into my palm. Stroking up and down, I felt his throbbing veins. We were equal parts aroused and terrified by the intensity of our need.

A surge of desire ran through my body. I wanted to possess him.

"Go slow, sweetheart." His voice sounded broken. When his fingers started traveling down and under my skirt, I pushed them away and he grunted again. "Why are you doing this to us, my love? I need you so badly. Please, stop this madness now." He was pleading with his words and with his eyes. "Look at me. Please."

I didn't slow down. Nor did I look into his eyes. Pulling my black lacy thong down, I adjusted myself around him. Then I took his cock inside until he filled me completely. He throbbed inside me. I was wet and so badly aroused that there was no resistance.

I had been starving for days.

I felt every inch of him. Inside me. Completing me. Vibrating from the shock, I opened my eyes slowly and locked them with his. Our chemistry hit the roof.

With his hands on my hips, he started setting the pace. We were hungry and desperate, but he must've forgotten that I was in charge. I pushed his hands away from me and moved at my pace.

He garbled something in frustration before his hand started roaming all over my bare back. He pushed his hips up into me; I arched my back. Unbridled electricity flowed between us. His every touch was stirring my senses and thawing my heart.

I was under a spell.

I desperately wanted to kiss him, to lie down with him, skin-to-skin, to talk to him and listen to him. But in the end, I simply fucked him. He filled me up so far and so deep, deeper than anything ever had. Milking his cock with all my might, I orgasmed in bouts of erotic pain.

When I was close to my release, Nick flipped us over and started thrusting hard. His heavy grunts matched my low moan. Our bodies were in perfect sync, acutely aware of another's needs and demands.

"I want you... with me..." he mumbled in my ear. "Ivy... give it to me." His thumb brushed my clitoris, circling it. "Now."

His thumb pushed and circled. I was lost to the pleasure, and soon, my climax brewed inside me. I didn't know what he meant, but he also didn't give me time to think or process. His expert fingers pushed in deeper, his hips snapping faster and faster. His teeth grazed my nipples. He found his own release, taking me with him. He shouted out my name, pulled me to his chest, and came inside of me.

We shifted our bodies in half a circle. We wrapped around each other and felt the hot, wild sensation coursing between us. A surge of electricity, a roar of our heartbeat, I wanted to submerge into him.

Nick propped himself up on his elbow, leaning over me. We waited for our breathing to even out, while his head lay on my shoulder. His breath seeped into my very soul. Wrapping my arms around him, I took everything I could. I didn't want to admit how much I needed him. My ego wouldn't allow me. My pride was hurt.

Soft lips made their way to my forehead. His hands traveled down my waist. He was still hard inside of me, filling me up. Like I was made for him, and he was made for me. He was reminding me of what this familiar, comforting connection meant to us. We were meant to be.

His lips trailed down my face. Right before his mouth reached mine, I turned my head.

"Maybe it's better this way," he muttered under his breath. Then he got up, withdrawing from me, leaving me hollow and empty. "I hope I was able to satisfy your needs."

Leaving me to my misery, Nick brought in a box of tissues from somewhere and put it down next to me. Then he got dressed without even looking my way. "Whenever you're looking for a fuck buddy, I'll be at your service. There's no need to come to nightclubs for that."

Tears stung my eyes. I was choking on all the words I

wanted to say. Cleaning myself off, I put on my panties, fixed my top, and moved toward the glass wall. I tried concentrating on anything other than the commotion inside my heart. Through the tinted glass, I saw the dancefloor downstairs. I knew no one could see us because half an hour ago; I had been one of many bodies down there. Even if they did, though, I wouldn't have stopped tonight.

It was just a fuck. I wanted to use his body, and I had. I'd wanted to hurt him for hurting my pride.

But in the end, I didn't get any satisfaction. I missed him so badly that my heart hurt. He was two feet away, but I couldn't take those few steps. Nick didn't take them, either. He was done with my rejections.

"Go back to Boston if that's easier for you."

His words cut me wide open. Shocked and speechless, I turned around and faced him. Tears trickled down, covering my already sweaty cheeks. "I thought you wanted me here."

"Yes. I wanted you to be with *me*. In *my* house," he seethed through gritted teeth. His shoulders hunched and he pointed his fingers accusingly. "I wanted to talk to Ryan and tell him that we wanted to be together. I wanted to tell my mother that no one could come between us. But you complicated everything. Your pride... you don't care about anything other than your pride and your ego."

Pain, hurt, longing—the range of emotions that I didn't understand, because once again, I was angry at him, and wounded by his words.

And I was mad at myself. There was no point in responding to him. No matter how much we tried, we simply broke each other more and more.

Chapter Twenty

It had officially been two weeks since I ended things with Nick. To my own surprise, time was going by faster than I thought it would. Work was getting crazier by the day, but I couldn't complain—I needed every kind of distraction I could get.

But the nights? My nights were hard. I continued with my runs until I exhausted my body to the point where I could fall asleep without thinking about Nick for hours.

Nightmares came and went. Running helped. When it didn't, Nick's voice pulled me out of the darkness. He was my knight in shining armor, my demon slayer, and he didn't even know it.

But he's also a controlling liar.

That little voice inside my head never forgot to remind me.

Who was Nick? I simply couldn't tell.

While I managed to keep my nightmares at bay, the assortment of emotions that surged through me with every picture of Nick and that perfect Sylvie Russo was beyond despair. He was constantly with her, yet I knew at the nightclub he only wanted me.

The paparazzi were all over him and his new girlfriend whenever they went to private romantic dinners. I burned with resentment. The only upside was that my name and face were nowhere to be found. I was finally old news, and I should have been damn happy about it, except I couldn't stand Nick's indifference.

After our encounter at the nightclub, he made no attempt to reach out to me. We were back to where we had been. He was distant, and I was hurting, silently longing for his touch.

Infuriated at not being able to get over Nick, I sent a message to the group chat I had with Cece and Risha: **I got an invitation to The Gotham Ball. Is it something worth going to?**

Although Rachael had encouraged me to go, I wanted more opinions. Cece replied instantly. *Absolutely!*

Risha quickly joined in. *Ryan and I got them too, but we won't make it. We are in Lake George.*

Cece didn't get the invitation, but she was curious about this ball. *Who are you planning to go with?*

I paused. **Dustin? Should I go? I hate the paparazzi were calling him my boyfriend at one point. Don't want to give him any wrong ideas or add fuel to the fire.**

A sign from the universe stuck on my phone. Cece and Risha sent identical messages at almost the exact same time:

Stop overthinking.

Stop overthinking!

———

As soon as I opened my social media app, pictures and videos of Nick filled my timeline. Tonight, he was at Tao with that freaking woman. At this point, Sylvie and Nick's relationship was longer than the one he'd had with me.

I resented her, loathed Nick, and smoldered with jealousy all at once. I was nothing but a dysfunctional, emotional cocktail. His new budding romance should've made me sad, but instead, I was mad. It also made no sense since I was the one who broke up with him, but reason had left me as soon as I got back to New York.

Deciding to spice up my life and get over his indifference, I called Dustin.

"Did you call to save my life?" he questioned, even before any pleasantry.

"What do you mean?" I spoke into the Bluetooth.

"I'm bored to death. France is so not for me." And for the next twenty minutes, he listed all the things he hated about France. I let him vent. It sounded like he needed it.

"So, why did you call?" he finally asked. "Missing me already?"

I rolled my eyes as I ran down eighty-fifth street towards Columbus Avenue. The sky was already dark, but I didn't want to go back to my empty apartment just yet. Burning with anger, I just couldn't let my mind go wild imagining all the things Nick was doing right now with someone who wasn't me.

Admit it. You're waiting for him to come back to you and apologize.

And that was the freaking problem. He wouldn't apologize.

"Hello? Did I lose you?" Dustin's voice pulled me out of my thoughts.

"Sorry. I was crossing the road. Are you still interested in Gotham Ball on Sunday?"

"Are you asking me out on a date, Ivy McAlister?" he teased, his tone laced with playful curiosity.

"I need a distraction and some good company," I explained.

"Are you sure there's no one else you'd rather go with?"

I wished, but no, there wasn't. I stopped at the light with a couple of other runners ready to cross the street and head into Central Park.

Since I had broken up with Nick at the Bethesda Terrace, I'd been coming here every night hoping to see him again. But knowing our history, and how selfish he was, I should've known better.

"I really want to go, Dustin. If you're seriously bored in France, can you come back?" This time, I literally begged him. That was how desperate I had become.

"I knew you couldn't live without me," he said, laughing. Still, it couldn't conceal the sounds of drums and singing in the background this time.

"Hey, isn't it morning in France? You're at a bar at this time of day, and I'm supposed to believe you're not having any fun?"

The pedestrian light turned on and I was the first one to step off the curb, and then a bright light flashed and enveloped me. Before it could completely consume me, an arm swiftly wrapped around my waist, anchored on my stomach, and pulled me back onto the safety of the sidewalk. My eyes flew open wide, heart pounding, to see a speeding car veering dangerously close. Tires screeched and time froze. The arm tightened its grip, yanking me further away from imminent danger. Adrenaline surged through my veins as the car wobbled and then drove off in a rush from the spot where I had just been standing.

"Careful, sweetheart."

Nick's scent traveled with the air, filling up my chest. I

closed my eyes, inhaling him, feeling his touch. His proximity. I turned slowly, feeling him in every fiber of my being. I could recognize his voice and his touch in my sleep. There was no one else who made me feel complete.

But when I steadied myself and finally turned to look, he was gone.

It took me a few seconds to understand what had just happened. In a black hoodie and a black cap, he was already running east. But he couldn't fool me. I could recognize Nick in a swarming crowd of millions.

"Nick, wait!"

He saved my life. Why was he running away from me?

He ran so fast that I was having a hard time catching up. He crossed street after street and then a few avenues. By the time I caught up to him, I was out of breath.

"Why are you running from me?" I clenched my stomach, face down, heaved for breath when we both stopped.

The man turned around. I look up. Instantly, heat rushed to my face and neck.

It wasn't Nick.

Embarrassed beyond words, I told the stranger, "I'm sorry. I thought you were someone else."

"All good!" the man said and walked away.

Was I hallucinating?

"Ivy, is everything okay?"

In the midst of it all, I had completely forgotten that I was still on my call with Dustin.

"Yes, I'm fine," I said. "I swear I thought I saw Nick, but it turned out to be someone else."

"You need to get over him already. He isn't worth your time."

"You're right." Leaning one hand against the concrete wall of a local pharmacy, I took a deep breath and tried to concentrate on the conversation before my imagination started running wild again. "Sure. France is not half as bad as you're making it seem."

"Seriously? I meant every word I said. Can you believe they're even opening up New York-style pizza joints? Copycats," Dustin complained.

I turned back and headed west, back toward my original destination. He kept talking until I told him I had to go. I couldn't concentrate on anything Dustin was saying because I was absolutely sure Nick had saved my life today, only to vanish moments later.

My mind started running a million miles an hour. Was he actually at a nightclub with another woman and I had simply imagined him? Or had he been going on runs with me all this time, and I hadn't realized it?

I could've called him and gotten my answers right there and then, but my pride was as gigantic as his ego.

Walking along the pillars of Bethesda Terrace, I circled the fountain until I was sure of my lone existence in this park. Then I got on the trail and walked until I reached Bow Bridge. I looked up at Nick's penthouse, its windows as dark as my tired and broken heart. I cried until there was nothing left and then I ran back to my apartment.

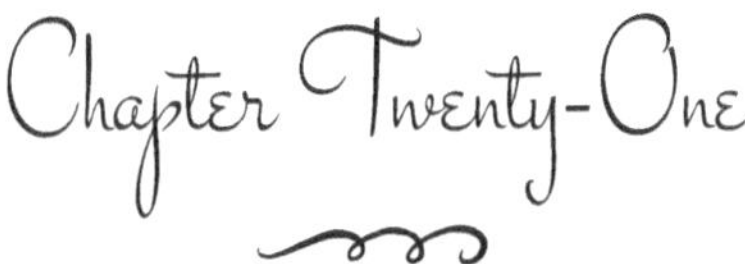

Chapter Twenty-One

s the sun began to descend on Sunday evening, the city pulsed with an energy typically reserved for the dawn of the weekend. Dustin and I exited our white stretch limousine and walked up the red-carpeted stairs.

If I had thought MoxTo's opening was overwhelming, the Gotham Ball was nerve-wracking. Photographers swarmed us, their cameras flashing like a swarm of fireflies, demanding poses and our best smiles until our jaws ached. Thankfully, no photography was allowed inside. I only had to fake it until we crossed the threshold.

I wore an emerald-green, off-the-shoulder silk gown with a daring left-side slit. Gold stilettos covered my scar and my stud earrings perfectly matched my dress. My hair was loose. Thanks to Cece and the ladies at the spa, my skin was rejuvenated like a newborn's. My face was a canvas for the makeup artist who made me camera- ready, a rare indulgence I thoroughly enjoyed.

Dustin wore a red tuxedo, adding a green bowtie to match

my dress. We knew getting all the details right was essential. The Gotham Ball wouldn't accept anything less.

As we walked in through the main entrance, a petite and friendly older lady in a black pantsuit asked if she should put my name down for something called "Bal-Din-Auc." Confused, I turned to Dustin, who was equally clueless. Several excited women around us added their names. I agreed and watched the lady scribble it down.

"You two are going to have a lovely time. Now, go in there and have fun!"

Another man in a black suit guided us to the Grand Hall, where an enormous crystal chandelier dominated the hall. Arched windows, closed for the occasion, were draped in rich, red velvet. The place was as elegant as the people who had gathered tonight. Plutocracy at its finest.

"You look sensational, Ivy. You fit right in," Dustin said, complimenting me, as multiple heads turned our way.

"I think it's your expensive French suit. You thought you could wear red and not stand out?"

He chuckled. "I specifically bought it for tonight."

"You look dapper," I teased, flashing him a smile. "Been here before?"

"Nope. My first time. Dad told me to go up to a hundred thousand for tonight's auction. It's for a good cause."

I stopped mid stride. "Auction? And you never thought of mentioning this before?"

"What do you mean? I thought you knew."

My mood soured. But Dustin was right. I had barely glanced at the invitation when it arrived. "Guess my budget should match yours, then? Do you think they take cards? I didn't even bring a checkbook." *What was I thinking? What happens during these balls?*

"Relax. We'll figure it out. Here, take this." He handed me a flute of champagne from a passing server.

"Look at us. Two rookies coming to The Gotham Ball," I exclaimed with a cheer. "Another experience to add to our list of adventures." We both started laughing, and my anxiety melted away.

Hanging out with Dustin had always been easy. From our first movie to secretly stealing liquor from my parents' collection, we had experienced many firsts together. Even though we hadn't met in years, we fell into our old routine at once.

The place was swarming with glamorously dressed people. I spotted celebrities, politicians, and business tycoons. But mostly, we didn't know anyone except each other. As time went by, I started getting comfortable. I didn't know what I was doing here, but it wasn't all bad.

An announcement echoed across the hall that the Bal-Din-Auc was about to begin and the participants should gather in the lounging room. Dustin wished me luck. Tossing down the rest of my champagne, I handed him my empty glass. I was ready for anything tonight.

———

"Miss McAlister. Would you like to go first, last, or somewhere in the middle?" As I walked into the lounging room adjacent to backstage, the same older lady from earlier in the evening approached me and asked.

Since I had no idea what I was getting myself into, I asked her to put me in the middle. She handed me a white sash with the number "Twenty-Two" written boldly across it in gold lettering.

I turned, attempting to step out of the line, and collided

with something hard. Instead of looking straight, my head rolled back to make sure I didn't fall on someone's dress. A hand grasped my wrist and pulled me forward. As soon as I had my balance back and was on my feet again, I looked up to thank my guardian angel. "Damien?"

"What a coincidence! We've been meeting in all sorts of places lately. Is the universe trying to tell us something?"

His beautiful smile caught me off guard. This was our fifth coincidental meeting since the nightclub, and each one had led to a lunch or dinner invitation. I made excuses every time, but he seemed persistent. Not that I didn't like him, but I wasn't looking for a relationship at the moment.

"It's always a pleasure to see you," he said.

"Likewise."

"Any chance you didn't bring a date and I can fill that role?" he asked, making a silly face that made me laugh.

"We're friends, Damien. And I am here with someone. Another friend," I clarified my intention, so there was no doubt left.

"Please don't put me in the friend-zone just yet. You're available. Give me a chance."

I raised an eyebrow. If he knew I wasn't with Nick, he must've been perusing gossip magazines and social media sites.

"I'm not looking for anything at the moment," I told him honestly.

"That's fine. I'll keep trying my luck until you change your mind."

I was about to tell him it would never happen; I wasn't attracted to him, but stopped myself. The Gotham Ball wasn't exactly the place for this conversation. "Are you here to grab a sash? I'm sorry to break it to you, but I saw only ladies there."

He chortled and then hooked his finger in the bottom of my sash to look closer. "Number twenty-two," he read out loud. "I guess I'll see you on the other side." Damien let go of the sash, winked at me, and left.

I stepped onto the stage with confidence, but instantly became nervous—and so I turned and left for the backstage area. Realizing it was probably too late to run, I found the old lady I had been talking to earlier.

"I'm sorry. What exactly are we supposed to do on the stage?" I asked, feeling stupid for not doing this earlier.

"Each woman will be auctioned off for the evening. The highest bidder gets to spend time with her. Proceeds go to a different cause each year. This year it's the Battered Women's Society."

What on earth have you got yourself into?

One by one, the ladies sashayed onto the stage, standing beside the auctioneer as the audience bid to spend the rest of the evening with them. Bids ranged from twenty-five thousand to a hundred thousand dollars. The entire process was weird and amusing simultaneously, but all the people, including the women on stage, were having a good time. Besides, it was for a good cause.

I soon realized there was no guarantee you'd end up with your original date, which added to the excitement. The auctioneer's humorous comments about every woman on the stage added a layer of playfulness. Number twenty-one passed me with a big grin. Her bidder turned out to be a construction tycoon turned reality-television sensation.

I stepped out onto the stage. Dustin gave me a thumbs-up. Knowing at least one person was looking out for me boosted my confidence. I hid my nerves with a broad smile and moved forward.

"Number twenty-two is none other than Ivy McAlister, in a beautiful Sahlene Couture." He nailed it, though how he knew, I had no clue. Sahlene Chu was new here but a sensation in Singapore, having only opened one boutique outside Asia, in New York City.

"Tonight is Miss McAlister's Gotham Ball debut. A New York native but new to town, Miss McAlister is a breathtaking gorgeous contradiction, and—"

"Two hundred thousand."

Everyone turned, shocked by the outrageous bid.

My heart stopped when I saw Nick. He was sitting all the way in the back with his auction paddle raised in the air.

"Two hundred and fifty thousand."

All heads turned to the other side of the room, where Damien had his sign up.

"Three hundred thousand," Nick countered.

The room fell silent. It was as if we were transported to London, caught in an intense Wimbledon match. No one knew how to react to this bidding war, including the auctioneer. I was way out of my depth.

"Four hundred thousand." Damien countered Nick's latest bid.

"One million," Nick announced nonchalantly, leaving everyone speechless.

Gasps and chatter filled the room. Nick and Damien locked eyes, the tension between them thick and palpable. Damien seemed ready to tear him apart, but Nick just shrugged, leaving Damien to simmer in his indignation.

The auctioneer hit the hammer, officially auctioning me off to the highest bidder. Dustin didn't even get a chance.

Chapter Twenty-Two

N ick and I met the old lady from earlier. I should've found out her name by now, but my brain wasn't performing at one-hundred percent. The ions in my blood were ready to burst forth, seeking their counterpart, and like a magnet Nick stood beside me. My entire being craved to lean into him, to mend with his presence.

I returned my sash and waited for the next instruction, trying everything in my power not to look at him. Not to give into my body's demand nor my heart's desire.

"You are one lucky lady," the woman said while Nick wrote the check. "We've never had a bid this high."

Nick leaned over the table and spoke to her. "I would've added any numbers of zeros necessary."

Her eyes glinted in excitement as she beamed with joy. I masked my nervousness with a meek smile. Nick stood up to his full height, took my hand, and laced it around his arm. Even in my high heels, I couldn't match his height. We walked to the ballroom along with other guests while his nearness, his obscene bidding, and his blatant display of possessiveness made my heartbeat run wild.

"What are you doing here?" I seethed when everyone was out of earshot.

"We're being cordial in public. Those were your exact words, if I remember them correctly." Nick nodded toward the dance floor. "Shall we?"

"What're you trying to prove to everyone, Nick?"

"I don't give a damn about any of them. Neither do I need to prove anything. You're all that matters to me, Ivy, and I'll die before letting someone else spend an evening with you."

"Seriously?" I glared at him. "The guy who is already with another woman is stopping *me* from spending an evening with someone else? You've got to be kidding me."

Nick held my gaze. My heart raced at an unnatural pace. The surrounding air crackled, and he pulled me toward him with an unseeable force. I looked away, trying to break the tension as we resumed our walk.

Why wouldn't he say he wants me, acknowledge his mistakes, and ask me to forgive him? And stop going out with that woman. Is that too much to ask?

I couldn't hold back anymore. I wanted the truth. "Are you sleeping with her?"

"Are you jealous, Miss McAlister?" His smug face was maddening.

I hated him so much. "You can only wish." *Crap.* I wanted to know, so I pushed further. "We had sex without any protection last weekend. I'm only asking because I don't want to get any diseases from you."

"Always thinking after the fact." His galling laugh burnt a hole right through my chest.

I hated this man and loved him with the same ferocity.

"Stay away from Damien, Ivy. He is not the guy you should get involved with."

"Jealous, much? I'm sure he can't be that bad. He doesn't try to control me like some people I know."

Frustration filled his eyes, so I pushed further. "And guess what? Said people don't even know how to apologize."

He straightened his back and took my hand in his. We moved toward the crowd without any further talking.

———

IN THE CENTER OF THE DANCE FLOOR, WE LOCKED eyes and took our positions. Nick placed his hands on my waist, drawing me closer. Heat cascaded from my waist down to my inner thighs, traveling further down my legs, burning my every pore. He was driving me insane.

He knew what he was doing. He enjoyed the effect he had on me. "Breathe, Ivy," Nick reminded me, dipping his head until his cheek touched mine.

I lost my last coherent thought.

"How long will you keep punishing me?" he asked, as his hands moved to my bare back. My skin reverberated from his touch. "Are you still waiting for an apology?"

He led me with finesse, covering the ground. Holding my right hand, he pushed me away, twirling me several times before pulling me close. I fell against his chest, inhaling his scent, and I closed my eyes against the dizziness I felt from his riveting nearness. Memories of our connection flooded back, reminding me of the emptiness since our separation.

"I didn't know how else to bring you back. I couldn't control your decision, Ivy, so I changed the decisions of those around you." He caressed my back as though he needed this contact more than his next breath. "I thought about us a lot these past few weeks and always reached the same conclusion."

When I met his eyes, the only thing I found was honesty.

"I'd do it all over again if it would bring you back to me."

I was losing my senses. Worse, I was losing myself. It was not an apology, not even close; but his sincerity spoke volumes. All the pain and suffering meant nothing compared to my feelings for Nick. I'd loved this man since the beginning. How could that ever change? The knot around my chest wasn't going away and the pain in my throat wasn't letting me talk.

"I can't stand this distance, Ivy. I'm ready to live with your anger, as long as you live with me."

His arms surrounded me. My arms were around his waist. We were not dancing to the music anymore, even though we were standing in the middle of the dance floor. The entire party ceased to exist. It was just the two of us. Nick and me.

I longed to forgive him, desperate to move past the hurt. Nick was my entire world. Without him, I had been incomplete. And now that I knew what being whole felt like, I wanted that feeling back.

"Tell me what you want, baby. I'll give anything to be with you." He cupped my face, his eyes pleading. "Come back to me, sweetheart. Please. I'm begging you."

Someone approached us, snapping me out of our bubble. I glanced around and noticed people watching us intently. Nick didn't care. His eyes remained glued to me. But over his shoulder, I saw Sylvie Russo.

He had come with her?

She tapped Nick's shoulder. Simultaneously, I pushed his hands off of me in disgust. My insides were gutted and raw, and I was in a whirlwind of emotions. He knew how to hurt me and, goddamn it, he had just done that again.

I walked away from them when they started talking. I

wanted to believe him when he said I was his and he was mine, but apparently his words and his actions did not match.

He rushed over, took my hand, and stopped me. "Don't forget, I've paid a premium to spend the evening with you," he said, his voice dropping to a dangerously low decibel level. His words were laced with menace, knocking the air out of my lungs.

"That's because you couldn't afford my company with your honesty," I shot back.

He glared at me, but stayed quiet. The sweetness and love that he had shown until a minute ago—it didn't exist anymore. Standing in front of me was the cold person who I had seen on the news, in magazine covers, and every time I hadn't fallen in line with his idea of our future.

Trying to pull myself together, I turned away and breathed through my mouth. I had to forget my feelings for him. I had to concentrate on the truth.

He was a liar.

A control freak.

And a cheater.

"You will get your money's worth, Nicholas Branson, and I'll make sure you're fully satisfied. Now, if you'll excuse me, I need to go to the restroom to freshen up."

My seething glare must've struck a nerve, because Nick sharply inhaled and released my hand. I fled the room, desperately needing distance to gather myself. His savagery had no bounds. His unpredictability knew no limits. His alternating hot and cold demeanor drove me insane, and once again, I blamed myself for not objecting when he lavished an extravagant sum on me.

All because I freaking craved him.

When I returned to Nick, I forced a smile—a requisite at these high-society gatherings I got myself into.

I spoke with every person who spoke with us and never left his side for a second. I kept one hand holding a champagne flute and the other holding onto his arm as he led me around the room. My new mission was to get through this awful evening without losing my mind.

———

We avoided personal talk for the rest of the evening. He never let go of my hand, even when conversing with the mayor of the city. But if I was cold, he was arctic. His intentions were so unclear that I had stopped making any sense of his behavior. I was simply counting the minutes until I could leave.

When we sat down for dinner, Nick pulled his chair closer to mine. We sat holding hands under the table, over his lap. Ridiculous as it seemed, it reminded me of our first night together at his house. A rush of memories flooded back— beautiful moments amidst the fights and arguments. A flicker of the best times with Nick by my side, a time when it almost felt like we were falling in love.

"It's good to have you back, Ivy."

I came out of my daze and looked up.

An older, elegant lady sitting two seats away from us smiled warmly. "I'm Anne Harrison, by the way." She extended her hand.

I put my fork down and shook her hand. "Good evening, Anne. Have we met before?" I asked politely.

"Anne is the wife of your company's CFO. You met Andy before we sat down for dinner," Nick told me, while nodding in her direction.

"Last time we met, you were a kid," Anne added with a

warm smile. "Nice to see you too, Nicholas. You both look beautiful together."

"Beauty is only skin deep. Besides, looks can be deceiving." I was not ready for people to assume we were together.

Her smile faded. She looked between the two of us, and Nick didn't even bother to respond.

Sensing the awkwardness and wanting no part of it, Anne said, "You look gorgeous in this dress, Ivy. It's your color."

"Oh, thank you—"

"She wears this color often, Anne," Nick said, his expression indecipherable. "It's her favorite color, but I can't figure out why." With that, he smiled before calmly going back to his food.

———

DUSTIN AND I MET AFTER DINNER.

"Let me know when you want to leave," he said, as he walked over to me.

"She is my date." As usual, Nick interjected. "I'll be taking her home."

"Nicholas paid a premium for tonight. I have to make sure I'm worth the money," I snapped, my voice dripping with anger. "Those were your exact words if I remember them correctly."

"How low do you think I am?" Nick's voice seethed with fury, ready to burn me down with him.

"Still figuring that out," I retorted. When I turned to Dustin, I realized that my fight with Nick was ruining his evening. Taking a deep breath, I softened my tone. "I'll call you tomorrow, okay?"

"Call me as soon as you get home." Dustin gave Nick a begrudging look before leaving.

All of Nick's focus turned to me. "Those petty pictures of you two won't make me jealous. I know he means nothing to you."

"Dustin means more than you ever will," I said, mimicking his irritation.

"Really?" Nick raised a brow. "Who exactly are you lying to?"

Unable to keep up the charade under his gaze, I averted my eyes. "At least he is an honest man who doesn't try to control me."

"If only someone knew how to control you," Nick muttered under his breath.

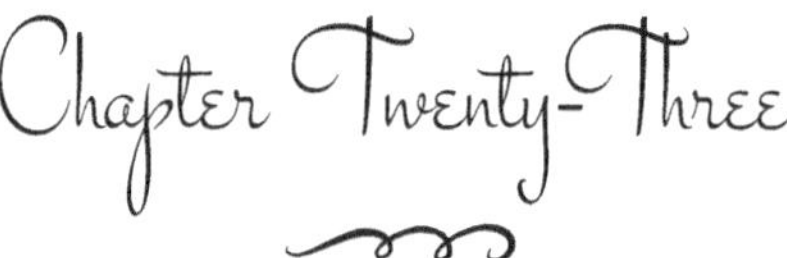

Chapter Twenty-Three

Nick and I joined the remaining guests on the grand terrace. For the rest of the evening we didn't talk to anyone, nor did we talk to each other. We held hands and wandered the rose garden, fingers intertwined, unwilling to sever our connection. We tried to prolong the night, fearing it would end once we left.

At times our eyes met, words forming but left unsaid... knowing they would lead to dark places. Together yet apart, we stayed silent.

I wanted to ask if he had saved my life that night, but stopped myself. He never gave me any indication. I also didn't see Sylvie Russo or Damien again. As always, only Nick filled my world.

When we left the terrace and went outside, the valet drove up in Nick's electric blue car. A young guy, almost a boy, stepped out of the driver's seat. "Roadster. What a car!" he said excitedly to Nick.

"Hope you had time to take it on a spin."

The guy flashed a smile to Nick, confirming he had done exactly that.

"You didn't bring your date in a limo tonight?" I said scornfully, unable to let it go. It didn't help that he had spent the entire evening with me. It also didn't matter that I was the one who had ended our relationship. Unreasonable, yes, but I still wanted him to be completely mine.

"Maybe I did. Maybe I didn't want to take *you* in a limo." He got into the driver's seat without waiting for me.

Not ready for a conversation, I shut my mouth and got inside. We were both to blame for our fights. The truth was, I didn't know how to talk to him without losing my restraint, either.

He started driving without asking where I wanted him to drop me off. That reminded me he was still tracking my phone. With everything going on, I had forgotten to reprogram it or get a completely new one. I got my phone out and started to look through it.

Accept it, Ivy. No freaking person has ever tracked your phone before.

As if reading my mind, Nick said, "You don't need to change phones. Just stop sharing your location. I can change the settings for you."

"No, thanks. I don't trust you with my phone anymore," I said, clutching it tightly between my hands.

"What is wrong with you?" he snapped. "You trusted me with your heart. With your body. Why can't you let things go?"

"Because you betrayed me! You wanted to control every aspect of my life. And as soon as we get into a fight, you go around with another woman as if... as if we never happened." At this point, I had no control over my emotions. The tears I had been holding back all evening came rolling out. It was all too raw. Being around Nick was too much to handle.

"What did you want me to do, Ivy? You abandoned the car when I asked you not to for *your* safety. I couldn't protect you when you went your own way. Ryan won't talk to me. What options do I have? The only way to protect you was to get the media away from you. I gave them something else to focus on."

I looked at him, confused. "What are you talking about? Who are you trying to protect me from?"

"As if you'll believe a word I say."

"I'm serious, Nick. Tell me what's going on."

"It doesn't matter. Tomorrow we'll be back on the front page of every paper again. Do us all a favor and stop using the subway. Stop going on your runs. Better yet, leave the city entirely."

"Only if you stop being an ass and talk to me. Is it the investigation? What has that got to do with me using the subway? You are not making any sense, Nick. Help me understand."

I waited for his response, for one that would melt my anger, one that would give me some perspective and make me understand his behavior... but it never came. Above everything else, his silence hurt.

It wasn't completely his fault. I also didn't know how to communicate without turning everything into a fight.

Nick parked outside my building and got out. Rounding the hood, he opened my door. When he offered his hand, I took it without argument. When he pulled me into a powerful embrace, I submerged into him.

My lips parted. He cut me off. "Don't."

Wrapping my hands around his neck, I leaned my head on his chest. He leaned against the car, taking my entire weight.

Time stilled. I breathed in his scent. His warmth enveloped me for which I craved. We were exactly where we belonged: with each other and lost in each other's arms. Our hearts started beating in unison. His lips stayed on the crown of my head. Selfish as I was, I didn't want this moment to end.

There were so many things I wanted to say. So many questions brewed inside me. I wanted us to find a way to be together again. I wanted the version of Nick who would listen and talk. The one who gave me my full autonomy back. I wanted *that* Nick so much that my heart ached.

All of a sudden, a hand started pulling me away from him. Shocked, I opened my eyes to see a fist slice through the air, slamming into Nick's face. My brother stumbled back, cursing.

"What the hell, Ryan?" Horrified, I tugged on Ryan's other hand. I wasn't sure what had gotten into him or how to stop this madness. When I looked at Nick, his lip was split. "Are you insane?"

Ryan turned and glared at me. I wish he hadn't. His eyes were filled with blinding rage.

"What were you thinking?" Ryan's words were laced with pure fury. Around us, lights turned on in windows in the apartments above us and in the townhomes across the street.

"It's not her fault, Ryan." Nick came between my brother and me, trying to shield me from his wrath.

"Yes, asshole! It's all *your* fault!" Ryan yelled, pointing his finger accusingly.

Worried that someone might call the cops, I tried to pacify the situation. "Ryan, please. Calm down. I'm not a kid anymore. Let me decide for myself."

"How well do you know him, Ivy?" Ryan's words stung like venom. "You come back here after so many years and think you know this world? You think you can deal with men like him?"

Taken completely by surprise, I narrowed my eyes at Ryan. "Seriously? You think I was living in some commune in the woods? You need to understand that I'm an adult now. Nick or anyone else, I know how to handle myself."

"I won't let you get hurt, Ivy." Ryan looked between Nick and me. "But believe me, you will. And when it happens, you will run away again."

"I will never hurt her, Ryan," Nick said, trying to reason with him.

"You already have. Don't you see that?"

It couldn't be any more painful than to see another person trying to control my life. Ignoring Nick, I looked straight at Ryan. "Let me learn from my mistakes."

"So that's how it's going to be?" Ryan's eyes squinted. Exasperation washed over him.

What happened to my calm and collected brother? Where did I lose that man?

"Fine." Ryan stepped back. "Find out for yourself, then. But don't say I didn't warn you."

I didn't understand what he meant, but he didn't stick around long enough to explain. Instead, he walked to his car, got in the driver's seat, and drove off, leaving me reeling from the shock and more questions.

When I looked around, the glow from at least a handful of windows caught my attention. A few people had even stuck their heads out their windows to watch the drama unfold. I took Nick's hand and went straight into my building, away from the curious, watchful eyes.

———

I DIDN'T LET GO OF NICK'S HAND UNTIL WE ENTERED my apartment. I took him straight to the living room and silently prayed he wouldn't have another scar because of me. I removed the first-aid kit out of a drawer and set it down on the coffee table. He sat down on the couch and I took a seat in front of him.

"You should see a doctor," I concluded, watching him wince as I dabbed hydrogen peroxide on his lower lip. "I hope it doesn't need stitches."

Nick took both my hands, head bowed. "I can handle any pain for you, Ivy. What I can't do is take away your nightmares. I'm dragging you down every day, aren't I?"

He reminded me of my long call with Abby this morning, who insisted I call Dr. Patrick. My most recent nightmare had been too intense and drawn out, and I knew something in my subconscious was triggering them. It could be this city or the mess my life was in, but it definitely wasn't him. "That's not true, Nick. You help me escape them."

"I'm also the reason they started again."

He wasn't completely wrong. I hadn't had nightmares for years, but as soon as we broke up, they started plaguing me again.

"I still want you back, Ivy. We belong together, and we both know it. I promise to shield you from your past, keep you safe, make you happy. Give me another chance, sweetheart."

I removed my hands from his and went back to cleaning his bloody lip. Slowly and diligently, I got rid of the blood and put some ointment on the cut. It wasn't as deep as I had imagined at first, thankfully.

"Your actions speak differently. I'm having a hard time understanding you," I explained.

His phone rang inside his jacket pocket, startling both of us. He swiped to unlock the screen and checked the messages instead of picking up the call. And then he got up from the couch. "Last time I told you the truth, you broke up with me."

"Last time, you told me you invaded my privacy and

interfered in every aspect of my life." I stood up, joining him. "And, yes, I want your apology."

Leaving me perplexed, he walked towards the door. *Would he rather leave than apologize for his mistakes?*

"I've learned my lesson, Ivy," he said. "That won't happen again."

"That's not an apology." He was at the door. I was running out of time. "Whatever is going on between you and Ryan, you need to fix that, too."

"Fixing things with Ryan is my top priority, but it's not entirely in my control. He's not talking to me." He checked his phone again, which hadn't stopped ringing. "I need you to go back to Boston right now."

Was he toying with my emotions again? The moment we start talking, he wants me to leave? "Why? So you can be with your new girlfriend?"

He faced me. "I'll find you when I'm ready."

"What's that supposed to mean?" My anger flared. "You go on with your mindless fuckery while I wait for you in Boston?"

He opened the door. "I can't be here. Go to Boston with John. Please, Ivy. Don't fight me on this."

"I won't go."

"You'll get everything you want."

What does that even mean? All I want is you, but not like this.

Frustration bubbled in my chest and rose to my throat. Nick was leaving me again. His phone rang non-stop, and he was already out through the door.

I rushed after him at full speed. "Did you save me from the incoming car that night during my run to the Central Park? Give me that much at least!" I begged.

"Yes."

And he was gone.

Chapter Twenty-Four

Despite the absence of sleep, I couldn't manage to unwind. It was Monday already. I got ready soon after Nick left and decided to distract myself with work.

When I saw my phone, I understood why Nick left so abruptly. Alerts filled my inbox with pictures of me and Dustin entering the ball, Ryan punching Nick outside my apartment building, and Nick and me entering through the door. The news of Nick's exorbitant auction bid created quite a stir. Now everybody knew my personal life and they couldn't get enough.

Calls from reporters jammed my phone. I muted it and stuffed it in my purse.

John was already waiting for me when I exited the building. I had no intention of getting into the car because Nick still had a lot of explaining to do. His commands weren't cutting it for me.

All of my stubbornness faded when I saw two reporters with long lens cameras approaching.

"Miss McAlister, you should get inside. Now." John opened the passenger door for me.

I jumped into the backseat and thanked him immensely. And I promised myself to never get annoyed when he showed up again. I also called Gwen, and it didn't surprise me when she told me to work from home and lie low for a while. I graciously accepted the offer, informing her I would work from Boston. She didn't mind.

I hoped it would allow me to get away from all the drama the media was creating. Hyping up every story, sensationalizing the news within hours in every news outlet... It was all too much.

"How long have you been working for Nicholas?" I asked John when we started our four-hour ride to Boston.

"Almost five years now. I'm part of his security team."

"Security team? I knew you weren't a driver. Were you protecting his other girlfriends, too?"

He paused. I let my words hang in there. I had too many questions and I couldn't wait for Nick's availability. "I served in the United States Marine Corps. Before joining the private sector, Captain Craig—the Head of Security at Branson Capital—was a marine, too. Our department handles all kinds of operational securities, but this is the first personal job from Mr. Branson," he said, enlightening me with a new set of information.

My heart leaped out of my chest, knowing I wasn't one of many. "Sorry for giving you a hard time. I was upset with Nick but I had no right to take it out on you. I was wrong."

"You don't need to explain, Miss McAlister. We've never seen Mr. Branson this worried before. Whatever you two are dealing with, I hope it works out."

"Me, too, John," I said, hoping. Contemplating. Sincerely wanting his words to come true.

———

AFTER DROPPING ME AT MY BOSTON APARTMENT, John reminded me to keep him on speed dial. He booked a room in the hotel across the street and gave me his full details. I wasn't sure if I was complying because Nick asked me to, or because the reporters scared the hell out of me. I wanted to believe it was the latter.

My apartment felt lifeless. Devoid of warmth. An alien planet where no one lived anymore. Abby was gone and everything was still packed in boxes, just as I had left it weeks ago. A lifetime ago. The new renters hadn't moved in yet but the furniture remained, so for now I had everything I needed to stay comfortable.

I stayed in, ordered groceries, cooked, and worked crazy hours. I also stayed away from social media because every trending hashtag involved Nick. His fight with Ryan was public news and though neither of them made a statement, the media wouldn't drop it.

I was caught right in the middle.

My biggest worry, though, was the investigation of Branson Capital, which was gaining momentum. Stock prices fluctuated wildly. The media bombarded Nick with questions about both his business ties to the McAlister Group and our relationship.

I winced, I cringed, I cried, and I sent countless messages to Nick and Ryan. Both ignored me until Nick sent me a single infuriating message.

Stay out of it.

———

I JUMPED IN MY SEAT WHEN THE PHONE RANG.

Nick? Ryan? Hope was all I had.

Dustin. I should've guessed. After all, he was watching the same news as everyone else. He was calling because he didn't like the media speculation about my relationship with Nick.

After talking for a good half hour, I asked him to drop it. "I don't want to talk about this anymore. First, I've got to fix things with Ryan."

"And you think Ryan will accept you and Nick being together? Your brother has taken a stand, Ivy." Dustin affirmed what I knew already.

"Stop, will you? I left because I needed a break. Now you're calling me to talk about the same shit?"

"Someone has to put some sense into you."

"And what makes you think I want that from you?" The last thing I needed was another Ryan lecturing me. Dustin wasn't the enemy, though. A concerned friend who was worried about me. His instinct to shield me from any harm came naturally to him because we had been close friends for a lifetime.

"Okay, listen. I hear you. I know you mean well. But right now I want to be alone and think for a while. Let me call you when I'm back in New York."

He stayed silent, making me feel bad for cutting him off. "When will that be?" he asked solemnly.

"Soon."

I had no desire to stay in Boston for years while Nick was with another woman. Neither did it feel right to stay away when he was under so much scrutiny. Going back, however, would mean living under a magnifying glass. I was stuck between a rock and a hard place.

I settled on the couch with a bowl of chicken noodle soup and placed my laptop in front of me. With social media and news out of my life, my distractions were limited. So, I searched for Damien Westford.

His pictures filled my screen. They were all great shots in various poses. After ten minutes of reading articles, I learned he had been a fashion icon until his father passed away five years ago. Damien then joined the family business, but things had been rough. His company, Imperial Portfolio Management, hadn't been doing well since Donovan Westford's death. Recently, a silent investor had acquired the majority of the company, and that was that.

Since the company was privately held, there was not much to go on. Frustrated with my lack of research skills, I shut down the laptop and picked up the TV remote. I browsed through channels until I found what I was looking for—the Big Bang Theory. Abby and my favorite show that we had binged watched several times. Today, it helped keeping my mind away from all the things happening around me.

"Is that truly you?"

Dr. Patrick Campbell got up from his chair to greet me. I had spent a substantial part of my teenage days in this very office, but it had also been two years since we last met. "I couldn't believe it when Monica said you called to make an appointment."

"Thank you for seeing me on such short notice," I replied, and a genuine smile spread across my face. I had called his secretary two hours ago and somehow she'd managed to squeeze me in. "You look great, by the way. Haven't aged a day since we last met."

He laughed modestly, settling onto the couch in front of

me. His tall frame, square-rimmed glasses, and neutral-colored shirt had remained unchanged for the past decade. But it was his warm, soothing voice that I had admired. A gentle nudge, a slight push. When he asked questions, I always wanted to talk.

"I celebrated my sixtieth birthday last weekend. My wife gifted me *disposable undergarments,*" he joked, making me laugh with him. His sense of humor was still intact. "I'm almost looking forward to my retirement now. But enough about me. Tell me why I have the pleasure of seeing you."

"Why do you think I need a reason? I just came to say hello." Now that I was sitting in front of him, I wasn't sure it was a good idea to be here.

"That's even better. Tell me then, how are things on your end? Still at Harvard? With the same boyfriend? Let me think... what was his name again?"

"Mike." My smile faded. "I've hurt his feelings in the worst possible way."

His eyes softened. "I hope you're not being too hard on yourself, Ivy."

"I should be, after all the mess I have created in everyone's life, but I've no control over..."

"Your heart?" He finished what I couldn't even after a minute.

"I've moved back to Manhattan," I blurted out.

"Oh, you have?" Without showing any signs of concern, he waited for me to explain. When I couldn't find the starting point, he only asked, "How do you feel about it?"

"Good and bad. Happy and sad." I knew I wasn't making much sense. I wasn't that same teenager anymore, so I should be more eloquent with my words.

I took a deep breath and let it out. "My nightmares are back."

"I see. And that's why you're here? Are they the same ones?"

"Yes. But something has changed." Without wasting his time or mine, I jumped right into the hard facts. From my initial visit to New York, to my breakup with Mike, and then Nick and everything in-between, I poured it all out. Like an attentive listener, he concentrated on everything I said.

When I finished, I let out my breath and realized I could breathe normally again.

"Nick…" He mused. "Isn't he the guy you ran away from all those years ago?"

I nodded.

He asked, "I thought you swore to stay away. How did he convince you in just five days?"

"That's the thing, Dr. Patrick. I can't stay away from him." My voice cracked from the pressure I had been under for weeks. It took everything inside me not to fall apart. "I tried as long as I could. No one completes me the way he does. Nick frustrates me with his chauvinist approach, but I don't know how to survive without him. I am disgusted with myself, but I can't get over—"

"Don't be so hard on yourself, Ivy."

"I don't know what to do!" Frustration brimmed over, seeping through my voice. "I go back home and my nightmares return. I want him so much that it hurts. Without him, life feels empty. Together, we fight constantly. I feel so confused all the time!"

"You have to fight your past at some point, Ivy. Running isn't a permanent solution." He paused, letting that sink in. "But if it gets tough, it's okay to step back and reassess."

Now that I was back in Boston, my nightmares had stopped. But was I ready to live a half-life just to be free from my past? We talked until the end of the session, and we concluded I needed to stay put in Boston for my sanity, at least for a while, until I could settle. He also wanted me to start my therapy again and ease into the change slowly.

But my heart was in agony. Indecision seemed to be all I had left.

Chapter Twenty-Five

On Friday, I told Gwen I would take the day off.

Other than the photo albums and some personal items, I didn't want to take anything back with me. By noon, with John's help, all of my boxes were in his car. I didn't know what I was going to do with my car in Manhattan. I couldn't take the subway or a cab and pretty much had to rely on a chauffeur. A few trips to the donation centers took care of most of it, and I ended up donating my car as well.

When Abby and Parker came to pick up her stuff, I had already taken care of mine. Abby and I hugged each other for a very long time. In thirty minutes, we were so deep in conversation that the men gave up on us and carried all the boxes to her car themselves.

Meanwhile, we sat on our favorite Adirondack chairs on the balcony one last time, and had our last coffee together in this apartment that we called home for the last two years.

After our initial catch-up, she jumped right into the pressing questions of the moment.

"Why didn't you call when you arrived?" Abby's jovial manner turned to disapproval. "You avoided my calls as well."

"I needed some time to think." With her, I was always truthful, and the truth was I needed time. To think. To feel. To make sense of the situation, I had gotten myself in.

"Want to share what's going on between you two? Not that I don't see Nick trending on social media all day long. But really, how is he, and how are you?"

This time, I told her about the conversation I had with Nick before leaving New York. How he had saved my life when I thought he was in a nightclub with his new girlfriend.

"Are you in touch with him?" I asked Abby. The only way Nick could have found out about my nightmares was through her. I hadn't spoken to anyone else except Dr. Patrick, who was bound by patient-doctor confidentiality.

"He texts me every day to check on you." Abby's revelation stunned me again.

"He doesn't respond to my messages." I heard disappointment in my own voice.

She picked it, too. Her shoulders sagged. "I'm sorry. I didn't know. He also told me you were in Boston. Since you weren't picking up my calls, I knew you needed space."

"Thanks, Abby." I meant it sincerely. "I really don't understand Nick. He says he wants me, but keeps me at bay. Tracks my phone and has John follow me everywhere. Asks you about my emotional well-being but goes around with another woman. What am I supposed to take from all this?"

"That woman is a distraction," she said, after mulling over it for a good few seconds.

"Why does he need a distraction? I clearly don't."

"You should let him figure out his mess before he talks to you. I don't doubt he wants you, but you're right, he's sending some crazy mixed signals."

"I won't wait forever. He has to come clean, stop going out with that woman, and stop spying on me."

"Yes, yes, and yes." She checked off imaginary boxes in the air. "First things first, let's get that tracking thing off your phone, I'm sure that's an easy switch that nerds like us should know, but we don't. Then give him an ultimatum because the fires of affinity are blazing brightly between you two."

"Fires of *what?*" I genuinely laughed for the first time in days. "That's the best you could come up with?"

"I mean it. Whenever you're together, you both clash. Whenever you're apart, you're both miserable. You need to find a middle ground or you'll burn each other to ashes."

Too stunned to speak, I let that sink in. Abby, a spectator and outsider, had summarized the essence of our imperfect relationship.

"Have you spoken to Ryan lately?" she asked, changing the course of our discussion.

"Ryan isn't talking to me anymore. He told me to stay away from Nick, and I didn't." I exhaled in exasperation. "And then this investigation, this freaking media storm... I'm losing my mind."

"No point in thinking about things that are out of your control. Be honest with yourself and answer the only question that matters: Do you love Nick?"

Abby's question didn't come as a surprise. All I had done since leaving New York was think about Nick and how I felt about him. My dreams, my reality—like always, they were only comprised of him. He was with me whether we were in the same room or hundreds of miles apart. He knew me like no one else did. And I was incomplete without him.

"I've so many unanswered questions, and yet I can't stop loving him. My heart hurts every day we stay apart, but I don't know how to be with him, either."

"Now you know how love feels. No reason. No fear of consequences. Forget Ryan and damn the media." Her grin widened with every word. "You are officially in love, my friend. And you need to fight for this love."

We both burst out in hysterical laughter. Until a few weeks ago, I didn't believe love was a real thing or it would ever happen to me. But, deep down, it was always crystal clear. Nick was *the* one for me.

When we got up to leave, I turned to close the balcony door. The sun hovered over the horizon, bidding me one last goodbye. The golden water of the Fresh Pond Reservoir tossed glimmering kisses my way. Today, my home for eight years, *my Boston*, was sending me off with a proper farewell.

———

THE YOUNG MAN AT THE STORE DISABLED THE location tracker on my phone. If I hadn't been drowning in a whirlwind of emotions all this time, and if I'd taken a moment to figure out a way forward, I could have ended this ordeal a while ago.

Since I wasn't ready to return to New York, and I had already bided my goodbye to Boston, Abby and I, along with John and Parker, drove to Marlborough. John gave me my space once I was at Abby's house and I promised not to set foot outside without him. Now that he'd started trusting me, I started liking him.

We got ready for a cozy dinner. Her family had always loved me and accepted me. It made me sad I wouldn't see them as often as I did in my four years of knowing Abby.

We dined and laughed and shared stories. After dinner, Beth, Abby's mother, handed us a list of groceries for Abby's goodbye barbeque. Her parents were determined to send her off on a high note.

———

Abby and I hit three different stores to complete our shopping list. John drove us around and helped us carry the heavy grocery bags. We invited him to the barbeque as a thank-you, and he happily accepted. Despite being an ex-marine now babysitting a grown-up, he remained dedicated to keeping me safe.

A small gathering in the backyard included our university friends and Abby's extended family, who I had become close to over the years. They were surprised to learn my true identity, the part owner of the McAlister Group, and my mysterious relationship with Nicholas Branson, the most eligible bachelor in the country. Everyone was speculating, and they all had theories. I had brought this on myself.

John watched me like a hawk. Knowing he had my back felt reassuring.

Half an hour into the gathering, I noticed Mike walking in. Blonde hair, blue eyes, and beard nicely trimmed—he hadn't changed much since we last met a month ago. Before my life took a one-eighty turn, I had liked him a lot; but loving Mike wasn't possible. Maybe that was why I hadn't thought about him since leaving Boston. How things had ended between us still haunted me, but I couldn't be his no matter how much I tried.

"How have you been?" He shoved his hands inside the pockets of his denim shorts and tried to act casual. I noticed his lips twitching, a nervous sign that appeared whenever he did something out of his comfort zone—asking me on our first date, going to our first movie, conversation about going exclusive, moving in together, our first time having sex. Predictable. Simple. A good-hearted man.

"Good. And you?"

"Not bad, considering everything." His voice tinged with resignation, making me wince inwardly. "You're becoming quite a celebrity."

I couldn't be sure if it was sarcasm or his pain talking. I saw him glance around. "He's not here, in case you're wondering."

His eyes moved to John and back at me. "Yeah, I noticed."

I should start with an apology. "I transferred to Columbia and moved into a new apartment," I said instead, desperately trying to fill the silence and search for the right words to atone for my guilt.

"New York suits you."

I bit the inside of my lip. "Mike, I'm... I'm truly sorry for the way things ended between us. It didn't have to be like that."

"There was no other ending for us, right?"

He couldn't hide the hurt I had inflicted on him. Behind all the sarcasm and snide remarks, he loved me. Unfortunately, I couldn't love him back.

"It was ugly and I want to apologize sincerely, but you're right. Whether or not Nick was in the equation, we wouldn't have stayed together for long. God knows I tried, but you deserve so much more than I could ever be."

A long, pregnant pause later, he spoke again. "Thanks for being honest. At least now I know where I stood in your life."

There was nothing I could say to make things right. So, I said the only thing that might clear my conscience. "I never intended to hurt you. I hope you don't hate me for the rest of your life."

"The worst part is, Ivy, I can never hate you. I wish you had stayed in Boston and given us a chance."

Mike and I had been together for two years, but that hadn't

been enough for me to forget Nick for even a day. We could've stayed together for another ten years and nothing would've changed.

"Now or later, this is where we would've ended up anyway. You probably don't see it, but it's better this happened now rather than later. I'm really sorry, Mike."

He winced at my words, and there was nothing I could do to ease his agony.

"I hope we can eventually get back to being friends," I said.

"I only wish you well, Ivy. But seeing your pictures with another man... I have to find a way to forget you first, before we can ever try anything else."

With nothing else remaining to be said, I nodded, hoping that things would get better between us someday.

———

THE GATHERING LASTED UNTIL LATE INTO SATURDAY evening, but I wasn't tired. I woke up early the next morning and helped with the cleanup. Once the house was back in order, I settled on the couch, tucked my feet under me, and decided to enjoy the beautiful New England Sunday.

Green grass, red roses, bees, and hummingbirds—the bay window framed a perfect morning. I had a bowl of cereal in one hand and my phone in the other. A typical summer vacation, which I hadn't had in a while.

The first alert on my phone was about me: "Ivy McAlister, on the run from Nicholas Branson," read the caption on a picture of me leaving the grocery store yesterday. Irritated, I deleted the alert.

More alerts flooded in. They were all about Branson Capital shares potentially falling along with claims that Nick couldn't run the company and shouldn't be the majority shareholder. Even after a week, the exchange between him and Ryan was still trending and dragging their joint investments into the spotlight.

It was all trash, but one alert caught my eye: Nick was meeting the press later today to make a statement. The mystery was killing me. How was staying away helping any of it?

After much deliberation, I called him.

Nick picked up on the first ring. "Ivy. Is everything okay?" His voice oozed with concern.

"Are *you* all right? What are these rumors about you and a press conference?"

"Everything is under control, sweetheart. Listen, I'm a little busy right now. Can I call you later?" Background noises made it hard to tell what was happening on the other end.

"I'm coming back to New York," I announced.

"Stay at Abby's. I'll call you later." Without waiting for my response, he hung up—and shut me off once again.

Not ready to let this go, I called the only other person who could answer my questions. Thankfully, she answered, even though it was the weekend.

With no time for pleasantries, I jumped right in. "Gwen! I need your help. Can you tell me what's going on with Nick's company?"

"Someone is out to destroy him and his company. It's getting ugly. That's all I can say." She responded immediately.

My stomach twisted in knots. "I don't understand. What has he done wrong? Who could be after him, and why?"

"That, I don't know. The investigation, him constantly being in the news, people questioning his capabilities to run the company—I believe there's something bigger going on."

"And that video of Nick and my brother that's circulating on social media?"

"False stories and AI-generated superimposed fakes. It's to

control the narrative and paint Nicholas as a bad guy." She spoke my mind.

"So, you're saying someone is trying to ruin him? On purpose?" My heart was beating fast under my ribcage. I was so busy mending my bruised ego that I failed to see the issues in totality. Nick was fighting a battle, and all I did was accuse him of something or the other.

"It definitely seems personal, Ivy. No one goes to these lengths to destroy reputations without a reason."

"Why is Nick not hitting back?"

Gwen exhaled. Was I asking dumb questions? I realized I didn't care what she thought of me. I needed answers.

"Whoever wants to hurt Nicholas also knows who his weakness is. Nicholas can't say much without getting into the discussion about you," she explained.

Had he been taking all the heat to keep me out of the media? I pressed further. "Nick and I met a month ago, investigation started around the same time. Don't you think it's too much of a coincidence?"

"I'm sure whoever is behind this has been planning it for months, if not years. It's the official investigation that started recently and that's when it became public news. If I had to guess, whoever is after Nicholas has found his pressure point and now they're riding high on it."

Like a puzzle, the pieces started falling into place. Why Nick stayed away from me, why he was going out with that woman... it all made sense. He was isolating me to keep me safe. Making sure John was always around, so he could fight the enemy without me getting caught in the crossfire.

All this time, he had been fighting the battle by himself and I... I had left him. My eyes prickled, but I pushed the tears back. I still had too many questions, but Gwen had given me the answers I needed for the time being.

"Thank you for explaining everything. One last thing, what time is the press conference and what is the location?"

"Ivy, don't go. Your being there will only make it even more of a circus."

I understood where Gwen was coming from and she might be right, but she was too late. My mind was set.

I hung up the phone as soon as she gave in and shared the details. Not standing by Nick wasn't an option anymore. Now that I knew the truth, I couldn't stand on the sidelines like a spectator. I had to act. And I knew exactly what I had to do to end this nonsense once and for all.

I begged John not to call Nick. To my utter surprise, he agreed. Thanks to his driving skills, we reached Manhattan's Financial District in a little over three hours.

I walked through the automatic sliding doors of Branson Capital's head-office and entered a massive lobby with black sintered stone floors, high glass wall ceilings, and heavy walnut security desks. Life-size screens on the central console showed real-time stock market news from around the world. It was Monday morning somewhere. The lobby was buzzing, even on a weekend, and security personnel and visitors clogged the perimeter.

I handed my driver's license to the first available security woman. "There's a press conference starting in ten minutes. I have to be there."

The woman nodded to John when he appeared next to me. It made sense; they were colleagues. The woman took one brief look at my license and called someone from her desk phone.

As I waited, I became acutely aware of my summery white

shorts and crop top against the pencil skirts and black suits around me. I had no plans to come here when I woke up this morning and after my call with Gwen, there had been no time to change.

"I really can't wait. It's an emergency," I reminded her, to speed up the process. Before I spoke again, a man in a black suit walked up to us.

"Miss McAlister. I'm Stephen, Mr. Branson's assistant." He shook my hand. "Follow me."

John and I followed.

People were making their way through the security checkpoint. Instead of joining the line, we were taken through another door into an empty elevator.

"I tried reaching Mr. Branson, but he must've already silenced his phone. He's probably heading to the media room as we speak." Stephen pressed the button for the top floor and took two steps back to where John was standing. I stood by the door. "You've access to the entire building, Miss McAlister."

"Take me to him, please."

"That's not possible," John interjected.

"He's right," Stephen agreed. "Building is swarming with journalists today. Mr. Branson wouldn't want them to harass you. I'll take you to his office."

"But..."

Stephen kept his eyes glued to the floor. I was pretty sure he wasn't ready to lose his job over me, so I let him off the hook.

When the elevator door opened on the second floor, I ran out and dashed into the elevator across the hall that was just about to close. Stephen and John lunged forward, dodging the man in front of them, but they caught up to me a second too late.

"Sorry. I promise, you won't be blamed for this," I said, just before the door closed in front of me.

———

ALONG WITH CAMERAMEN AND A SOUND TECHNICIAN, I entered the crowded room. It was a scene straight out of a movie. The press briefing room buzzed with anticipation, a dozen reporters jostling for position. I stood in a corner like a mere spectator, unnoticed by people engrossed in their own individual conversations.

The noise faded when Nick entered the room and took the podium. His hair was neatly brushed back, complimenting his signature black three-piece tailored suit. He exuded confidence, like he had nothing to worry about. His team—a group of men and women in tailored suits and pointy stilettos—followed him and stood a short distance away.

"Branson Capital is a diversified holding company whose subsidiaries engage in investments, portfolio management, real estate, and hospitality," Nick started, wasting no time. "Recently, we have also diversified into exceptionally profitable venture capital. Each subsidiary is exceedingly profitable on its own, which collectively makes Branson Capital among one of the largest publicly traded companies in the country."

The people in the room were hanging on his every word. And so was I.

"Today, we're gathered to discuss the investigation into our investment and portfolio management operations. My team and I have willingly cooperated with any requests we have received until now. There is absolutely no evidence of anyone here committing a crime.

"I'm sure you're all wondering why this investigation started in the first place. We will get to that eventually; I promise you that. When will this investigation end? Well, your guess is as good as mine. But like I said in my statement earlier

—we have nothing to hide. Let the authorities do their due diligence and let the truth come to light.

"Until then, Branson Capital stands by its principles. We will continue to cooperate with the investigation as we have been doing so far. We base everything on ethics and honor here at Branson Capital. We will continue to do so no matter what," Nick concluded.

A pin dropping could have been heard in the room as he finished his statement. A pillar of strength and the face of Branson Capital, Nick was always in control of his fate and the successful business empire he ran. A bogus investigation would not shake him, and he wanted the world to know that.

Debra Tomar from the *New York Times* was the first to ask a question. "What about your hospitality business, Mr. Branson? The one you're partnering with your close friend, Ryan McAlister. Should investors be worried about your strained relationship?"

"Investors have nothing to worry about. There has been no change in the way we conduct business," Nick replied.

Another reporter spoke from the other side. "Is it true you're planning to sell a portion of your shares?"

"I have no such plans." Nick responded, calm as ever.

"But what do you have to say about the investors' fears, Mr. Branson? You can't deny that the drama surrounding you is affecting the company negatively."

"My personal life is exactly that—personal. We have more well-known business executives in the country with a lot more drama going in their lives."

Muffled laughter drifted through the room before someone said, "So, you agree you are in the middle of your own personal drama, Mr. Branson?"

"Next question, please." He looked at another reporter, who had his hand raised for a while. "You," he invited.

"What would be your response to the accusations of fraud that have been circulating for weeks now?"

"Every accusation is baseless until proven."

Debra cut in before Nick could call on anyone else. "If the accusations are as baseless as you claim, then why was the investigation started on Branson Capital? If shares fall, what will you do to stop the downward spiral? Do you have anything to say to your shareholders?"

"Shares will stay stable. If you don't agree, we can talk tomorrow after the markets open. I would also like to point out the facts again. We have been fully cooperating with the investigation. So far, they have found no foul play and they never will. Our last nine quarters have shown solid growth and this quarter will be no different." Nick's response was strong and poignant, shutting everyone down. Or that was what I thought.

"What do you have to say about your fight with Ryan McAlister?" another reporter asked. "The videos and headlines are pretty scandalous."

Nick glanced around the room until our eyes met. His demeanor instantly shifted from the poised master of his universe to a concerned man. Worrying about my safety and wanting to keep me out of the spotlight had gotten him here today. No way I was going to stand back and let these reporters grill him further.

One cameraman noticed me and turned his camera.

"That was a private matter." Nick brought the attention back to himself. "It has nothing to do with Branson Capital."

"Isn't it true your aggression toward Ryan McAlister caused his sister, Ivy McAlister, to leave the city?" The annoying reporter spoke again. Ryan's slap had split his lips, but the circulating video told a completely different story after being doctored. Though his lips had healed now, but that slap still resonated in every conversation. "If this is how you are in your personal life, how can you expect the shareholders to trust that you can successfully run a multi-billion-dollar company? Maybe you should consider giving away the majority shares of Branson Capital to someone more capable. And maybe get a better CEO for this company, perhaps."

The room fell silent. The reporter smirked, sensing he had the upper hand here.

Nick's calm voice stopped all the murmuring in the room. "You're trying very hard to make a personal matter very public, Mr.–"

"Scott Anderson," the reporter responded.

"Mr. Anderson. Let's discuss my capabilities after the quarterly earnings report," Nick said, hardening his eyes.

"You keep avoiding questions about Ivy McAlister, Mr. Branson," Scott Anderson pressed on.

"Someone is feeding you misinformation to discredit Branson Capital. I'm not sure who is behind these rumors, because I'm here," I spoke up, firmly.

The murmuring grew louder. As I walked toward the podium, all eyes turned to me. Nick, downright surprised by my courageous act, kept his gaze fixed on me. I walked up onto the stage, stood beside him, and covered the microphone. My next words were for him only. I whispered, "We're in this together."

Shocked, surprised, elated, upset—it was hard to tell what went in his mind because his face remained impassive. But immediately the course of the interview changed and the reporters started questioning me.

"Are you confirming your romantic involvement, Miss McAlister? Everyone wants to know what happened that night between you, Mr. Branson, and your brother?"

"Like I said, this is a private matter," Nick told the

reporter. His voice was sterner. "If you have nothing meaningful to ask, this press conference is over."

Before I could fully comprehend, Nick's hand was on the small of my back and ushering me toward the exit. I was on a roll however, and I desperately wanted to end all the speculation. I turned around and said, "If you're that curious, the answer is yes. We are romantically involved."

Microphones were thrust into our faces and cameras flashed, momentarily blinding us. Nick wrapped his arms around my back, shielded me as we quickly exited the room and escaped from the media circus.

———

"WHAT ON EARTH WERE YOU THINKING?" NICK demanded. We had just entered a large conference room on the other side of the building, surrounded by his entourage. "I told you to stay in Boston. Why can't you ever listen?"

I couldn't tell if he was annoyed because I defied his orders, or angry at the reporters for asking invasive questions.

"Didn't you see? They were trying to discredit you over a stupid fight between two friends. How could I do nothing when they were turning you into a bad guy?"

"That's not the point, Ivy. I was handling it."

"Now we are both handling it. Together." I raised my chin and took my stand.

"Well, everything's out in the open now." Brian Koschitzky, Branson Capital's CFO, spoke up. I recognized him from The Gotham Ball. "Ivy is right. This could be a great thing. Let's wait for the eight o'clock news and see how the market reacts tomorrow morning."

I hoped Brian's words would convince Nick, because the irritation on his face and his tensed jaw hadn't diminished. I still had hope since more people joined the wagon with Brain, thanking me for intervening and analyzing market's reaction.

"Can everybody leave this room?" said Nick. "I need a word with Ivy in private."

Apparently not.

———

THE DOOR CLOSED WHEN THE LAST PERSON LEFT, leaving us in an uncomfortably silent room. A long table stretched between us, emphasizing the grandeur and power of the place. Through the glass wall, the concrete jungle of the city stretched endlessly. Yet the man inside the room commanded my complete attention.

Outside, Nick was a powerful figure, someone people feared and respected. But here in the conference room, his intensity was tempered.

Or so I thought.

"Do you realize what you've done?" Nick asked curtly.

"The media will stop talking about your fight with Ryan. If I had to, I'd do it again."

Nick rubbed the back of his neck. "Media will start hounding you more than ever. Your private life won't be private anymore. You do realize these reporters are very good at twisting facts to come up with stories that sell, right?"

I shrugged. "Nothing new. They're doing that already."

"If you thought *that* was bad," he said, inching closer, "now it'll be a hundred times worse."

"It's still worth it. I don't want you to explain yourself to them."

Nick reached me and gently brushed my cheek with his thumb. His demeanor softened, and butterflies returned to my stomach. "Ryan will be furious when he watches the news."

"You and I have some work ahead of us." I leaned into his touch, feeling his palm against my cheek. His warmth trickling into my skin and calming my nerves.

"We can't even talk to each other without yelling, arguing, and breaking up."

"I agree. You should work on your communication skills."

Placing his hands on my waist, he laughed aloud for the first time.

My heartbeat sped up from the sound of his voice filling the room, resonating within me, and traveling to my every pore. I narrowed my eyes at him. "Are you seriously finding this situation funny?"

Closing the remaining unbearable distance, I wrapped my arms around his neck. This closeness was what I needed. He was everything I ever wanted, and I refused to let him take all the heat in order to protect me.

"All I can do is laugh. Otherwise I'll drive myself insane." He tugged me gently, his expression turning serious again. "Ryan is going to be very upset, Ivy. This exposes you to unwanted attention. Media got a piece of you back there and now they'll want more."

"We'll talk to Ryan. Make him understand we want to be with each other. And I know you'll protect me." I was speaking rapidly, like a bullet train, but I needed to say it. "I love you, Nick. Don't push me away. I can't stand being apart from you anymore."

He locked eyes with me, and I saw it again. Love. Adoration. Gratification. "I want to apologize for all the mistakes I made. Hurting you was never my intension. You've no idea what you mean to me, Ivy. I've waited my whole life for you. You have the power to make me the happiest man or break me to nothing. Promise me that whatever happens, you won't leave again. Give me your word."

"I promise you, Nick. But you have to meet me halfway and let me in. I want you to be honest with me. Whatever happens, no matter how bad, you have to tell me everything. No more secrets."

He nuzzled my neck, attraction humming in every inch of our existence.

"No more secrets," Nick whispered. His face dipped and his mouth claimed mine, his warm tongue stroking deep and fast. Our kiss filled with urgency and hunger. I was his once again, and pleasure surged through my body as he pressed closer.

"Take me home." I whispered into his mouth.

"Yes, sweetheart. It's about time."

THANK YOU FOR READING FIRES OF AFFINITY! I would really be grateful if you could leave a review on the platforms of your choice. Your reviews are my tips to bring in better books next time.

Much love,
Delia

Read on for a look at the third and final book in Delia Duke's Intertwined Series:
Bonds Unbreakable

Nicholas "Nick" Branson:

"Ivy is The One... my deepest desire, my sweet obsession, my grounding anchor. She was the forbidden apple I could admire but never have. So, I had let her go, convincing myself we were better off apart.

But when she returned to Manhattan, it jolted me out of the life I'd been coasting through, proving how wrong I was in letting her go. I want her in my life, defying all the odds stacked up against us. With the vultures circling overhead and my ship sinking faster than I could comprehend, I just couldn't let her go or consider moving on. My fierce need to protect her from all powerful forces-external or within. I want her...at any cost."

Ivy McAlister:

"Nick is a force of nature, my guiding star, my soulmate, and the eternal object of my desire. I thought he was a control freak when I broke up with him, only to discover his immense need to protect me has no bound. He fights all his battles alone to keep me safe, but how can he protect me from my nightmares within.

Money, power, position breed countless enemies and Nick has a few of his own dark hidden truths. How long can he protect me when everything around us is falling apart faster than the life we are building for ourselves?"

Join the mailing list to be the first to preorder Bonds Unbreakable.

Website: https://www.deliadukebooks.com/
Instagram: https://www.instagram.com/deliadukebooks/
Facebook:https://www.facebook.com/deliadukebooks/

Acknowledgments

To my husband, Sonny, you have been on my side at every step of the way. Without you, my dream would have only been a dream. Thank you for putting up with me and picking up slack when I am in my zone. (All the time). One day, I will make you read my book as well. It's a hope.

To my daughter, Tyra, for patiently waiting for my attention. There are times you have survived on Z-bars because Mumma was busy writing. You took everything in your stride. I hope you learn the power of grit. Finish what you start and never look back.

To my editors Ieva Ulozeviciute, Janeen O'Kerry, Shane, and the entire team. Without your hard work and support, this book wouldn't have seen the day of light.

To my friends and beta readers, Piya, Amy, Sarada, Swas, and Becca, without your feedback, this book wouldn't have been as complete.

And the last, but not the least, my readers. Thank you for coming along on this journey with me. For trusting me to deliver you something that you enjoyed. I look forward to our long relationship here on.

About the Author

A new and upcoming author, Delia writes contemporary romance with a deliciously stubborn alpha male, strong female, and plenty of steams and angst.

A travel enthusiast and a foodie at heart, she loves incorporating her life experiences into her stories and will never say no to girls' night out.

An analyst by day and a writer by night, if she is not working, you will find her traveling the world with her family or eating out with her friends.

To know more about Delia, please visit her website @ https://www.deliadukebooks.com/

* 9 7 8 1 9 6 5 0 0 6 0 4 7 *